# TALES

# OF A

# MINSTREL

## TALA BAR

Acknowledgment is made to the following publications in which the stories in this book have appeared: "Death and the Minstrel" in *Unlikely Stories* and *Pens on Fire*; "Minstrel in the Forest" in *Bewildering Stories*; "Dragon's Flare" in *Nanobison* and *Peccary*; "The Water Nymph" in *Scribal Tales*; "Dragon Ride" in *Scribal Tales* and *The Cynic*; "Through the Circle" in *Static Movement* and *Mung-Being*; "Music, Love and Magic" in *Scribal Tales*; "Winter on the Mountain" in *Scribal Tales*; "The Magic War" in *Orion's Child*.

To my editor and publisher, Mark Givens, who had first published some of my stories in his online magazine MungBeing, and now is producing this book; without him I would not have been able to make the product of my mind presentable.

ISBN: 978-1-938349-00-3

Library of Congress Control Number: 2012915411

*Book design by Mark Givens*
*Cover photography by Tala Bar*

First Pelekinesis Printing 2012

www.pelekinesis.com

# Tales of a Minstrel

by Tala Bar

# AUTHOR'S INTRODUCTION

Finbar the Minstrel appeared one day out of nowhere in the "feverish mind" (as the Hebrew saying goes) of a writer struggling to find her way between concrete reality and imaginative fantasy. He was made as a real man belonging to the real world of supposedly European middle ages, trying to make sense of some fantastic ideas, that pestered him but also enriched his hard and severe existence. Out of this combination of reality and fantasy I hope I managed to create a world that would entertain and enrich the open-minded reader.

*Tala Bar*
*June 20, 2012*

# CONTENTS

# DEATH AND THE MINSTREL

## I

Finbar was very ill. This time, he thought, he's not going to get out of it. In the past two years he had been frequently sick, mainly had stomachaches sometimes accompanied with fever. As time went by it became worse, and he was going through attacks which, with their passing, left him feeling worn out, lifeless, with no energy to do anything.

But this attack seemed to take longer, would not pass after the initial day or two. He was lucky not to have had it when he was alone on the road by himself, where no one was to care for him. He had already been two days in the village before it occurred, entertaining the villagers with his stories and songs. They had fallen in love with them, as usual, and were ready to take care of him when he was taken ill.

Finbar woke up from a disturbed sleep, burning and shivering with high temperature, his body twisting with wave after wave of recurring pains. The people of the house the Minstrel was staying at took turns in looking after him, putting cold poultices on his head, washing and trying to feed him at need.

"You're so good to me, Martha," he whispered on one such occasion to the face peering at him for a moment out of the thick fog, in which his mind had been swimming; he had to make an effort to give the right name to the face. It was a good face though not particularly pretty, round and white like the Moon, the eyes shining at him almost like silver. Their goodness had reminded him of his elder sister, who had taken care of him as a child. He was back to that time now, when he had taken advantage of a slight cold so that Ronna would spoil him, and he could avoid going out for his regular chore – herding the couple of cows she had managed to save for the family. Hers was not a light job, after their father had left the family never to return, and their mother always ill, especially in her head. It was Ronna who had taken care of the rest of the family – some five or six children, he could not remember now – as well as the house and the farm. It was lucky for them their elder sister was the person she was.

• • •

Finbar did not dislike herding the cows; actually, it was his favorite chore, as it enabled him to roam the wild pastures, at least while the weather was fine with no rain or snow. It allowed him the freedom he had yearned for so much, before he upped and ran away to become a minstrel. He had loved his elder sister, and was even ready to take her with him; but at that time she was already married, with one child and another on the way. And, anyway, her sense of responsibility had always been too great to ever abandon those who were dependent on her.

It was Aile who would have gone with him, if she could. She was two years younger than him, pretty and wild, her body still as flat as a boy's, unlike the gentle, round-bodied Ronna. As much as Finbar liked Ronna best of all his siblings, Aile liked Finbar best; she had always attached herself to him, neglecting her own chores in order to accompany him to the pasture, telling him her imaginary stories. Indeed, she could have been a minstrel herself, as good as he had ever been! Why couldn't they run together, she would say, roam the roads, visit the villages, sing and tell their tales? She had so many of them, the product of her weird brain!

"Girls do not roam the roads," he used to laugh at her.

"I'll dress as a boy," she argued – her arguments had always been so rational, even when they had no sense at all.

Poor Aile! She fell ill that memorable summer, even as his own plans to run away were taking shape. She raved in her fever, spoke non-stop about wandering in the fields, busy doing what she liked best – gathering little kids, with two or three adults joining them for a lark; they would do it underhand, ashamed of being attracted to a young girl's follies – granting them a taste of her made up fairy tales. Finbar would have stayed behind when Aile fell ill, he did not want to leave before she got better; but she never did, and her little grave was one of the things he had left behind, one of the memories forever coming back to haunt him, and one of the sources for his never ending tales.

# II

Martha came and put another cold compress on his feverish head, and the sick Minstrel felt again a touch of his elder sister's hand. He loved Ronna so much! Sometimes, while growing up, it might have been the kind of love forbidden between sister and brother. He remembered Ronna blossoming into womanhood, getting rounder every day, her body filling up in various places, her breasts forming into two eye-piercing fruits – those forbidden fruits from the Garden of Eden! How did he yearn to cup them in his palm, kiss the full lips, interlace his legs with hers... In a strange way, the burning fever flared his withered loins, of which he had not made use for years...

As Martha was bending over him, he stared at the image growing before his eyes; he saw the woman thinning up, her body twisting around his in a snake-like shape, her head elongated and her mouth opening to reveal a pair of fangs.

"Who are you?" Finbar asked, shivering with cold and fear.

"Don't you know me?" it hissed at him; "don't you recognize the figure of Death of Sins that prevented you from sleeping with your sister?"

"You are Sinful Death!" the Minstrel cried weakly in his alarm, then mustered his courage and replied, defiantly, "But I have never committed that sin! I never slept with Ronna!"

"Sometimes thoughts are as bad as deeds," the snake uttered, "I've come to take you to the place from which you can never return!"

Finbar's head fell back on the pillow and he shut his eyes. "I don't care, everyone else is dead, anyway..."

"No," hissed the snake, gradually retreating back into the womanly shape of Martha; "I'll let you be this time, because you don't care enough for life anymore…"

"What are you saying, Minstrel?" Martha asked, full of concern. But Finbar fell back into his disturbed, feverish sleep, to the wild dreams that were pestering him.

This time, the image of young Ronna was replaced by that of his mother, always sick, sometimes a little mad. The birth of each child made her more and more ill, until her husband could take it no more and took off, and she herself sunk into a mental and physical depression. By the time she reached forty, she looked like an old, crazy hag, who sometimes lay on her bed for days on end, and other times roamed the village aimlessly, muttering crazy sayings no one could understand.

That was how it looked to Finbar now, in his feverish dream. Suddenly, it was a bright, sunny day and he saw himself as a boy of eleven, half watching the two cows in the pasture, half looking away at the green hills surrounding the village, with dots of flowers strewn in them. A song stirred in his mind and he was humming to himself, when a shriek pierced his ears. He turned to look and saw that hag, his mother, dancing wildly outside the village, her arms spread wide to her sides. Under the tatters she wore he could see parts of her thin, wrinkled body, and as usual he felt ashamed of her appearance. He started walking in her direction when she began to transform. Her body got thinner and thinner, shedding parts of flesh together with the scant garments covering it; from under it, bones peeped out, taking a greater and greater part of the body until nothing but a skeleton was left, dancing on the green hills. The boy Finbar stood still, leaning on the long stick he always used to chase the cows with, scared out of his wits at the sight. Gradually, the skeleton came nearer, until it stood in front of him.

"Hi, Finbar," it said in a grating voice, "leave these miserable animals; you're coming home with me, now."

"Who are you? What have you done with my mother?" asked Finbar, his voice shaking.

Bursting out with a horrible laughter, the skeleton replied, "But I am your mother, Finbar, I am Mother Death!"

"You are not My Mother!" he shouted back, his whole body shuddering with fear and rage. "Go away!"

Laughing and shouting, the skeleton started another dance around Finbar, its bones rattling, threatening to fall apart. Finbar, feeling sick, raised the long stick, and shook it toward the apparition. "Go away! Go away!" he cried, his voice full of tears of terror and sadness.

• • •

"Minstrel, Minstrel," a soft voice penetrated his dream, shaking him gently out of his terror. He opened his eyes and saw Becca, Martha's daughter, her lovely young face bending over him, half-covered by a halo of golden-silver hair. "Have you had a bad dream? It must be the fever. Here, I brought you a broth the healing woman made for you. I'll help you drink it and it will revive you."

She helped him to a half-sitting position, took the wooden bowl in her hand and brought the wooden spoon to his mouth. But his throat burned too much to swallow, and the liquid dripped down his neck. Weakly, he shook his head, and she put the bowl down on the little sideboard beside his bed. "We'll try later, then perhaps we'll wash you, so you'll feel more comfortable."

She left then, and he returned to his dreams, seeing her as a princess with golden-silver hair locked in a tower, waiting for the cruel dragon to come and devour her, as it happened in some of his tales... He was walking along with his bag on his back, telling himself one of the tales he used to tell his audience on dreary nights, to shake them into a pleasant fright before going to sleep in their warm, comfortable beds. He had just left the village he had been staying at and was going in the direction of another, passing through a dry and deserted countryside.

An unexpected sight appeared before him, a high tower of whose existence in that place he had no idea. Its blank walls had no windows, and immediately the thought of the beautiful Princess locked up in it came to his mind. At the same time he recalled the Dragon for whom she had been waiting, trembling with fear, and the brave handsome Knight that must come to save her... Finbar looked around him in search of this knight, when a sudden idea leapt to his mind. Was not he, in fact, that very knight who was going to save the Princess and win her love?

He heard the noise then, something between a growl and a shriek, and he knew the dragon was coming to claim his catch. Finbar pulled out his sword – of course, he had a sword, more like a knight than a minstrel, for whom a sharp knife had always been enough. As he prepared a stand against the beast, it appeared before him, a huge creature all fiery red, dotted with black and yellow spots that enhanced that terrible image. But the monster, instead of approaching the tower, headed straight toward Finbar himself! Why was he doing that? How did the tale go wrong? The creature opened a huge mouth, from which flames burst out, scorching the Minstrel's hair and heating up his face.

"Hey, Dragon," he dared shout with a scant breath, "aren't you making a mistake? Aren't you supposed to attack the girl in the tower?"

"No, Finbar," the beast roared, "it's your turn to die now, and you can't escape this time!"

## III

"I'll save you, Finbar," he suddenly heard an old, grating voice, hoarse for the many tales he had told and many songs he had sung in his life. Turning in surprise, Finbar saw his Mentor, the Old Minstrel who had been dead for many years. Here he stood, as large as life and as young as he was when Finbar had first met him. The Old Minstrel had been visiting Finbar's village on his wanderings; all through that night, fifteen-year-old Finbar listened to the words and the music when everyone else, including the storyteller himself, had been falling asleep. The next day it was when his young sister Aile suddenly fell into the sickness, of which she died within three days. The Old Minstrel, sensing Finbar's feelings, stayed until it was all over; he then took him with him to roam the roads, never to return home again.

"You can't save me from the Dragon, Master, you're dead yourself!" Finbar protested, feeling himself trapped between the dead and the deadly.

He recalled now the years he had been wandering with the old man, learning the profession of a minstrel. He learned how to gather and preserve everything he saw and heard, shaping the raw material into proper forms, which he sang before an enchanted audience. He learned how to keep his audience charmed, so that later he could get his food and a place to sleep at night in exchange for his songs and tales. After the first few months the Old Man had let him do his part in the entertainment, and gradually, as the Mentor was getting older and weaker, his student was becoming stronger and surer of himself. Finbar began using his own material, both what he had miraculously found in his head, and what he recalled of his dead sister Aile's stories. Sometimes he felt as if she were coming back to him, finding room in his own mind, from where she was enriching the treasure of his tales and songs. Her inventive power had been greater than his, and he learned how to use this power for the benefit of his trade.

One morning, having stayed at night under a big old oak tree on the side of the road, Finbar woke to find the Old Minstrel dead. Without much thought he found a shallow hole in the ground, in which he put the body, covering it with a few stones and erecting a cross he had created out of two wooden sticks. He did not say a prayer on the grave, only a few words of farewell, took what he found as valuable from the old man's sack, and went back on the road. Again, as when he had left home, he never looked back.

"You can't fight Time, boy," the old man said to him gently now, stretching his arm to Finbar, "come with me, I'll take you home."

"No, no, no!" Finbar cried, trying to run away as was his wont. "It's not my Time yet! Death as a Friend cannot take me more than Death as an Enemy!"

• • •

The scene dissolved around him, and he went back to his sleep. Uncounted figures from his tales and his songs came up to surround him, and he stared at some of them, talked to others, regarding all of them – the pretty girls and the old hags, the weird monsters and the funny creatures – as his friends of all time. Then Martha came back, her Moon face engulfing him with its kindness.

"Lie quietly now; please don't get so upset," the Moon-face said to him as it peered out of a layer of the fog that surrounding it. But it looked different now, gradually enlarging to encompass the world. It emitted a bright white light which blinded his sick eyes, and he shut them tight.

"Who are you?" he asked in a whisper. "You're not Martha, where has she gone?"

"Martha can't help you any more, Finbar. I've come to take you with me," sang an enchanting voice from the light.

"You're my sister Aile, aren't you? I haven't seen you for such a long time, I've almost forgotten…"

"Yes, dear Finbar. But now, we need never part again. Come, let's leave this miserable world and go over, to the Light."

"But you're dead, Aile! Where can you be taking me?"

"To the land we all go when our life is ended, Brother. Come!" The bright figure of light stretched an arm of light and touched Finbar on his forehead. The Minstrel felt himself lighten up, with no more pain or heaviness. Slowly he rose and followed the bright figure, not looking back to see his inert, dead body lying on the bed.

• • •

# DRAGON'S FLARE

"I don't believe in dragons!" cried a young man of the audience, after the minstrel had finished his tale.

Finbar laughed, wryly, "Neither do I, really. It's just a tale, my young friend. You should enjoy hearing it, not necessarily believe in it." A few minutes later he followed his hostess to her house, where he would spend the night before continuing on his way.

The morning lighted on a pleasant autumn day, and he was all set to travel the short, day trip to the next village. Finbar was in a good mood, and nothing was going to disturb it for him! As relations between the two villages were cordial, there was a clear path to walk on. The area was hilly and slightly rocky, with a few trees growing sparsely here and there, their leaves getting colorful red, brown and yellow before falling; the grass underfoot was yellowing as well, after a relatively dry summer.

The minstrel was whistling to himself as he walked, his sack on his back and his coat on top of it, his long staff in his hand, being sometimes used to lean on, but now he waved it in the air in rhythm to the tune he was whistling. He was looking around him gaily and curiously, when he suddenly stopped. Up above, at the top of one hill higher than others, a strange rock reared its oddly shaped form. It was quite uneven, serrated with protrusions here and there, giving the overall impression of the head of a dragon...

Dragon! Finbar inhaled, closed his eyes then opened them and looked again. It really looked like a dragon, though he was sure he had never seen a dragon in his life. Nor, as he assured that young man in the village, did he really believe in their existence. But here Finbar felt the need to be a little careful. He indeed had encountered some strange creatures on his roaming ways that he hardly believed existed outside his own tales and songs. Now, dragons, surely...

By now, the thing's shape had changed. It moved, and it grew taller, as if the dragon was standing up; a pair of enormous wings appeared on both sides of the strange head, moving and flapping with a great noise. The rocky creature then took off, flew up and circled a few times, then started going down – down – getting closer and closer to Finbar and becoming huge in the process.

The Minstrel was standing, nailed to the ground, unable to move. The dragon hovered for a few minutes above his head as if studying his appearance; then, slowly and gradually, it folded its wings and landed, right beside Finbar. The Minstrel, who had held his breath until then, emitted a long breath and breathed in again, deeply.

"So, you are Finbar," he heard a rumbling voice emitted from the direction of the dragon.

He was now forced to look at the monster, just to be polite. It was so big that Finbar was unable to grasp its whole figure at once. It was certainly bigger than the largest animal Finbar had ever seen, perhaps twice as high, much wider and very long between the tip of its head and the end of its tail. The latter was moving restlessly to and fro, giving the minstrel the feeling of immediate danger and he tried to move away from it. In these few moments Finbar had a chance to look at the dragon's appearance, and was amazed to notice that, though it was scaly according to the best of stories, its scales, which looked as if they were made of copper, did not lie flat but were standing on edge, seemingly bristling. Each of these coppery bristles reflected the low rays of the rising sun, and Finbar was not sure if it made the dragon more or less frightening. It certainly gave it a look of unexpected, bizarre beauty. In addition, from among the spiky scales on its head shone a pair of the clearest green eyes he had ever seen. They reminded him of a woman he had met some time ago, in very different circumstances, which he could not recall at that moment.

The Minstrel felt the need to be polite, at least for the purpose of averting danger, so he asked in his gentlest voice, "Did you speak?"

"I was just making our acquaintance," the rumbling voice resumed, and the minstrel noticed a light orange-tinted smoke flaring out of the monster's nostrils.

'It is breathing fire,' Finbar thought, fleetingly, his heart racing, and answered in a trembling voice, "Yes, I am Finbar; and you are?"

"We'll leave that for later. Right now, I have come to help you in your coming trouble."

"What trouble?" The idea made Finbar less aware of the danger emanating to him from the dragon itself.

"Here it comes. Just step behind me and you'll be all right."

"Why should I step behind you when I see nothing in front of us?" Finbar resisted the suggestion. But then, he saw it too. From behind a hilly fold in the ground, a row of flickering spear points appeared. Behind them, rose helmets that shone in the sun, and soon a whole body of marching soldiers were seen, advancing right on Finbar and the dragon. The beast spread its wings and rose in the air, looking like a mass of shining copper points.

"Don't worry, I'm here with you!" the rumbling voice sounded like drums in the minstrel's ears, as the body diminished in size. Finbar turned his eyes from the dragon toward the approaching soldiers who, in quite a short time, stood before him.

"Hey, man, what are you doing here, all on your own? Aren't you afraid? There is a war going on, and you are right in the middle it!" A man addressed him, a big body mass, heavy and strong, a head taller than Finbar. This must have been the commander who, instead of a spear, was carrying a large club, with a short sword hanging from his belt. Finbar had met military men before, as individuals, but never in such threatening circumstances.

"I haven't heard of any war," Finbar answered. As a wandering minstrel, he knew his way around people and had never been afraid even of the strongest and most violent of them. But he had never met them in such a mass that made them look like an enormous monster, no less intimidating than the dragon. He lifted his eyes for a second to see where the creature was.

"Some baron is going to war, and you should join one side or the other to keep safe, and not find yourself between two warring armies."

"But I am a minstrel!" he protested. "I wander about and do not belong to any baron, nor am I interested in fighting."

The commander laughed, with his men joining him in a roar. "Interested? Who is asking you? You're coming with us, to become one of us and fight for our baron, and if you do not come willingly, you'll come by force." He signed to the men, and two of them stepped forward. "Take him!"

They just stretched their arms at the minstrel, as a great roar sounded from above, and a mass of coppery spikes fell on the men. Finbar could not say they were frightened away, because a shower of spears flew at the dragon. But the dragon shook these off and started spewing flames, scorching the soldiers. They were lucky to be wearing helmets, Finbar thought, before he felt arms seizing him just the same, using his body as protection against the monster. But the dragon waved his enormous wings, and his spiky scales hit at the men, forcing them to drop the minstrel and scatter away. The dragon roared and rumbled again, throwing flames after the escaping soldiers, until none of them were left around. Then the monster lifted and was gone, and for a few moments Finbar was alone among the rocky hills.

He shut his eyes for a moment and fell to the ground, catching his breath. "Did you get a good fright, then?" he heard a laughing, clear voice that did not belong to the scene he had just experienced. He opened his eyes and immediately rose to his feet.

"Where did you spring from?" He asked the lovely woman standing before him. She was dressed in a copper armor made of spiky scales, and under her copper helmet, from among a bunch of coppery curls shone the loveliest pair of green eyes he had ever seen...

"But you must know me as I have just saved you from a fate worse than death," she laughed.

"Worse than death... Well, I wouldn't argue, but thank you all the same. Still – what about the dragon?"

"Well, it's useful, don't you think? I could not scare them away in this form, could I?"

• • •

# MINSTREL IN THE FOREST

## I

The Minstrel reached the forest toward evening, having walked all day. The weather had been fine, fairly clear with a few white clouds sailing in the blue sky; but now the clouds grew heavier and darker, as if in response to the dark lump that loomed before him, in the shape of the forest that filled the horizon; he saw no break through which he could pass into it. Finbar knew this forest had a bad name. Hunting in it was usually unsuccessful, and if an animal would be caught, it would usually prove to be unsuitable for any human usage. On the other hand, such would be hunters that tried to brave the forest were many times come to grave harm themselves, injured or even killed in the act.

Finbar had no intention of hunting. He was not a skilled hunter, did not like to kill living things and preferred other kinds of food. But he was curious, and had always been ready for any kind of adventure that occurred on his wandering way. The forest was there for him to investigate, and that was what he intended to do. He was not too hasty, though, to confront any danger with a brave heart, and he had always been guided by caution.

This forest looked really threatening, like no forest he had ever seen before. The trees that stood at the edge were tall and dark, the branches in front stretched forward like menacing hands that guarded the entrance; those that stretched sideways interlaced from tree to tree to create a wall of tightly close network. Finbar wondered how he could overcome such a formidable obstacle and get into the forest.

As evening was falling, the Minstrel knew he was too tired to try anything now; instead, he looked for a suitable spot to camp for the night. He found a nook between two rocks jutting out of the ground, and saw he could hide there from the stirring wind. He collected a few stones and arranged them in a circle, gathered some dry twigs and lit a fire to warm his tired limbs. Sitting by the fire, he took out remnants of the food he had received from the landlady at the last place he had visited; she had also filled his leather bottle with ale, which he now sipped with pleasure.

Though enjoying such visits with people, who paid for his tales and songs by fine hospitality, Finbar also loved his own company. He now relished the peacefulness of the darkening twilight and, having finished eating, he wrapped himself well in his coat, stretched on his back with his head resting on his bag, and looked at the few stars peeping out among the heavy clouds. "Once upon a time," he started telling himself one of his many tales; he hummed an accompanying tune to turn it into a lullaby, thus softly putting himself to sleep. Finally, he closed his eyes and slept.

• • •

A strange growling voice broke into Finbar's slumber. "Hey, Minstrel, are you asleep? Come, let me show you my kingdom – isn't that what you've come here for?"

Finbar opened his eyes. Instead of the dark night that was taking over the earth when he lay down, gray twilight now covered the earth, creating dark silhouettes of the objects around him. Among the shady figures of the trees, the shape of an enormous bear took form in front of his eyes, filling the Minstrel's heart both with fear and a sense of adoration. Its fur was light brown with golden highlights, and the hair on top of its head stood in the shape of a crown. The only thing that softened the apparition a little was its pair of greenish-brown eyes that seemed incongruously kind in such a menacing appearance.

The figure spoke again, its groan rolling like a muffled drum; its words, however, were clear enough. "Come, wake up, Finbar, let me show you my forest," it  said in a commanding voice.

Finbar sat up. "Your forest?" he asked. "But who are you? What are you?"

"I am Bear, King of the Forest." he said; "you must have heard of me in all those myths you tell people."

"I didn't know the forest had a King?" said the Minstrel in wonder.

"Someone has to take care of what happens here, as anywhere else," Bear said with a great deal of self-importance. "Now, are you coming? I can't wait for you forever."

"Yes, of course I'm coming," Finbar replied, shaking off his apprehensions. "I'm always happy to make new acquaintance, whatever it may be."

He rose to his feet, shook the dirt off his clothes and picked up his sack; after dispersing and crushing the last embers of the fire, he followed Bear, who had turned to go among the trees. For a moment the Minstrel wondered how they would be able to break into the solid looking grid created by the trees; these, however, were nothing now but the shady forms of their earlier nature, and the two of them passed through as if the trees were nothing but gossamer. With a flutter in his heart Finbar followed Bear into what he knew to be a threatening realm; then he remembered that his guide was King of that realm and he must trust him to help and protect him against any evil that might be lurking in the forest.

For a while they walked in silence, passing easily through the vague shapes of trees and shrubs. Gradually, a weird thought appeared in Finbar's mind that either he and Bear, or these parts of the forest, were ghosts, not real, physical creatures. How else could this strange walk happen?

It was still the same gray twilight all round them. The trees stood erect, seemingly frozen in the very still air; they were no longer solid as he had seen them before he had fallen asleep; Bear and Finbar also met many animals on their way, but they were nothing like the beasts he knew must roam a forest, but looked strange and deformed. They stood around in silence just like the trees and shrubs, neither trying to flee nor to attack them.

"I don't understand," the Minstrel said after a while, "they don't look like real animals. Shouldn't I be afraid of those great teeth and claws?"

"No," replied Bear, "because you're right. They are not real but the spirits of the animals which had lived in the forest a long time ago."

"Ah!" Finbar emitted, staring around him in silence. He wondered about these strange, transparent beasts that lived a long time ago, and the ghostly trees and shrubs that surrounded them, and thought he was never in his life going to see such weird sight again.

"I am not sure I could ever tell about them to my audience," he said at last to Bear, doubtfully.

"I am not sure you should, anyway," the creature replied, "they are not like the myths and tales you usually tell them about, and they would not understand."

"No..." agreed Finbar, slowly. "Let's go on. Aren't there any other things to be seen in your forest?"

On the whole, he was not completely sure whether he was still dreaming by the fire at the edge of the forest, or whether everything was really happening. For a time, the Minstrel had decided to suspend his faith in anything he was going to see and experience.


## II

"Grannie," said the young girl, "is there any world outside that forest? Sometimes I feel I absolutely suffocate here, and I would like to see something else beside trees, shrubs and beasts." She was just beyond puberty, her feminine body barely formed; she had long, straight, fair hair and dreamy sky-blue eyes, and she was clad in a leafy yellow-green cover.

"You know, Nimmi," replied the old woman, who had a bent back, long white wispy hair and deep black eyes, "I am so old I can't remember. You'd better ask Mother." She pulled a little nervously at the brown-gray sack that covered her shriveled body.

Mother, a tall woman in the prime of her life, had reddish-brown hair falling to her shoulders in heavy waves; her eyes were sparkling greenish-brown and her full mouth red, and she was wearing regal-looking deep red robe. "I am not sure you should ask such a question, Nimmi," she said in a soft, sensuous voice, the effect of which was lost on her daughter and mother. "And you should not encourage her, Grannie," she added, with a tinge of severity in her voice.

"I have a feeling," the old woman croaked, "that we are going to have a visitor very soon. I suggest we go hunting in his honor."

The other two were not in a habit to question Grannie's "feelings"; they prepared for the hunt though it was not one of the seasonal occasions when they usually had meat, in addition to their more regular vegetarian food. Nimmi took her bow and quiver of arrows off the branch they were hanging on; Grannie began sharpening her knife on a strap of leather tied to another tree; and Mother prepared the fire in the midst of a stone circle.

• • •

A sudden glitter appeared in the gray forest through which Bear and the Minstrel had been walking. There were flashes of colored lightning in red, green and yellow, that surprised and alarmed Finbar and he stopped and called out, "What are those?"

Bear stopped as well. "Ah, I see they're coming. I'd hoped we'd have a little more respite."

"Who is coming?" asked the Minstrel.

"I didn't want you to meet them, it could be unpleasant, but they are not actually under my control, not exactly being part of the forest."

"So there is some present menace in this forest which you neglected telling me, is there? What is it, then?" the Minstrel asked with a trace of sarcasm in his voice. Later, he would be sorry for this attitude of his toward Bear, who had been only nice to him.

As the flickering lightning drew nearer, they stopped walking, and after a while, Finbar saw vague figures among the flashes of lightning. Gradually, the figures became more definite, and at last he was able to discern two beings in female human form, one very young and one very old. The Minstrel threw a questioning look at his guide, and was surprised to see Bear growled unmoving; it just stood there, growling, causing the Minstrel to feel the Mother King itself was showing unexpected fear. If such was the case, what was he, a mere human to feel or do?

In the meantime, Finbar took this break in action to examine the two female figures.

The young one looked ready for hunting, with the bow and quiver of arrows slung over her shoulder. She was almost pretty but not quite, still immature in body and her face too determined to be beautiful; but she looked subtly impressive in her readiness for action, with her long, fair hair flying about in the light breeze that was suddenly blowing, and her long legs under the short, greenish-yellow cover; her sky-blue eyes looked at him with strange interest, is if he was some kind of odd animal to be hunted. His heart gave a momentary flutter to that thought, and he turned his gaze toward the old figure. That one much more frightening than the other, and he did not really want to look at her; he felt her deep black eyes piercing his soul, and the word Witch came to his mind at once, though he had never met an actual witch beside the usual village healer or wise woman.

After a while, as if to relieve the tension that was created by no one speaking, Finbar said aside to Bear, "they look solid enough, not like those trees and animals from the past."

"They are real indeed," Bear answered; "I only hope you won't have to find out how much." With these words, the Minstrel sensed a shudder racing along Bear's body, which seemed incongruous with its huge entity.

Before he had a chance to ask more, the old female croaked, "All right, Bear, we are taking over now. You can go."

"Where is Mother?" he asked in such a fierce voice that Finbar had not heard it use up till now.

"It's me and Nimmi today," the old Witch uttered. "You've no say in the matter, you know."

"One day you'll be sorry for it," Bear warned, but to the Minstrel he said, "I've tried to avoid this, I'm sorry. I wish you good luck..." It then turned and slipped among the forest trees, vanishing as if turning into a ghost like one of them.

• • •

After Bear was gone, though, the forest was no longer the same gray, transparent mass as before; the trees and shrubs had become solid again, standing very close to each other to form one dark green block; its menacing atmosphere had returned, and the Minstrel's heart missed a beat once in a while, his limbs shaking as if he was freezing cold. With a dampened spirit and a sense of doom he tried to avoid looking at the two women, who were looking at him so intently. His mind froze, and he could not imagine what they had had in mind for him.

From under half-closed eyes Finbar sent a glance at the old woman, who seemed to have sprung straight out of his classical tales as an authentic witch. She had begun behaving in a very witch-like way. Humming what sounded like an enchantment, she started moving around in circles, in a most horrible, crooked dance. It made Finbar dizzy, and he felt he was unable to move away. He shut his eyes with terror as he felt a sticky, invisible spider web forming around his limbs; it held his arms tight to his body and his legs planted in the ground. More and more threads were wound around his body until he could not move his head, and they filled his mouth until he could not utter a sound. At last, he felt as if an unseen shroud was wrapping him, trapping him like a cocoon.

Then, like in a cocoon, he felt a strange restlessness in his limbs under the web, as if they were changing their shape, as a caterpillar changing into a butterfly inside the pupa. Slowly they altered, his arms lengthened until they reached the ground and turned in legs, his legs shortened to become of the same length, his body bent to accomplish his new form, and his head grew larger and his nose longer, becoming a snout; for a moment he thought that perhaps he had been turned into a bear. Then, as his new shape had been completed, the web slowly melted away; Finbar's body was released and became flexible and movable again. He opened his mouth to talk, but could only emit a kind of snort, and a huge pair of tasks jutting out of his snout gave him the right answer. Carefully, he opened his eyes to take a look at himself. Smaller and grayer than a bear, with that pair of tasks, he was confirmed in his suspicion of having turned into a boar.

Unable to speak, Finbar sniffed in fear. He looked, bewitched, at the old female, who had now stopped her circling around him and burst with a wild laughter. The hair of his fur stood on end, and Finbar Boar started skipping on his short legs, shrieking in high snorts and calling for help. But the more he shrieked, the more the Witch laughed.

The girl joined her now, giggling and calling out, "Ah, Grannie, you've done us proud." She drew out an arrow from the quiver on her back, checked its point then positioned it on the string of her raised bow. "Run, Boar, run!" she cried out loud. "I know you understand my words, and I want you to give me a good chase for my effort to hunt you!"

Finbar, stunned, stood motionless, unable to move even without the wrapping of the web around his body. 'Hunt! Me? A human being and a respected Minstrel?' But he could not voice these words aloud, and his heart sunk to rock bottom.

"Yes, Yes, Yes!" Grannie answered his unpronounced thoughts. "The quicker you run the longer you'll stay alive, so do us and you this favor!"

Something in the old Witch's voice made Finbar snap out of his paralysis. He lifted the boar's short legs and started running. 'But what about the trees blocking his way,' a fleeting thought passed in his still human brain. Strangely, those threateningly solid trees did not seem to block his way, and he passed through them as if they were still in their ghostly form. For a moment his thought turned to Bear, who perhaps could come and save him. Then another thought came up, explaining Bear's existence as that of the Spirit of the Forest. It seemed to have no power against the wicked Witch!

Who was she, then, to be more powerful than the forest itself?

But there was no time for thinking now. He was running for his life and he'd better make the best of it! So, Finbar Boar ran on, leaping and skipping as he had never done in his life, feeling the danger chasing behind him. A sharp pain in his backside told him that danger was very real, when the girl's arrow punctured his skin. Stunned for the moment, he turned the head to look behind him, and was able to make out the shape and colors of the young creature named Nimmi, flying like the wind among the trees and shrubs. 'Like a Nymph!' the thought came flying into his confused mind; but he knew he could not pause to reflect, as he would do in his human shape of a minstrel. So, he ran on and on, forgetting the pain he had in his fear for much worse, hoping against hope that his short legs would hold until salvation came, if ever…

# III

"Stop!" A commanding voice penetrated through the fog gathering in the Minstrel's tortured mind. It took him some more hurrying paces and a little more time before he was able to bring himself to a standstill, gasping for breath. He turned to look, and a strange vision encountered his misty eyes. The chase had stopped in the heart of the forest, with the tall, dark trees standing all around them Finbar and Nimmi, with the Witch coming flying at them from lagging behind.

Now, however, there was another figure among them, a third woman. Nimmi, still holding her uplifted bow with the arrow poised on the string, was standing still, her sky-blue eyes full of suspicion. Beside her the old hag was dancing on crooked legs, full of hot protest. Between the two, full of such a majestic air with which she was controlling them, stood a tall woman as beautiful as Finbar had ever seen. Through glorious, thick, reddish-brown wavy hair surrounding her finely-carved face, a pair of greenish-brown eyes shone at him. For one moment he could not recall where he had seen such eyes before.

"You'll have to stop this game, the two of you!" she told the other two. "Enough is enough!"

"No!" cried the old Witch. "We're having fun and I don't see why we shouldn't have it any more."

"Even though that's the reason humans shun us and don't want anything to do with us? No, we should never hunt humans again, and perhaps then we can show the people we are able to benefit their lives instead of harming them."

"But how would Nimmi be able to practice hunting?"

"She can hunt real animals – they expect it! You have no need to use humans for that practice!"

"But it's much more fun hunting humans, Mother," Nimmi intervened, but she lowered her bow and put the arrow back into the quiver; "they are much more intelligent than real animals, you know, which makes it more fun!"

"You'll have to have less fun and hunt just for our meals now, Nimmi," said Mother, severely. "We can find fun in having real relations with humans, instead of this cruel treatment of them. You asked why we have to live in the forest and never go out, and that's your answer."

'Ha,' Finbar thought to himself. 'What have we got here, then? Good material for a new story?'

"Oh," the Witch stopped her dancing about at last, saying with a tone of resignation, "I suppose we have no choice, Nimmi. Times have changed, and we can do nothing about it. What d'you think we should do, then, Mother?"

"First of all, turn this man back, Grannie. Let's take a good look at him and find out what he's doing inside the forest. He must be an unusual human to be here at all, without you having to kidnap him from the village."

"I didn't kidnap him from the village, Mother," Nimmi answered; he was inside the forest with Bear." Grannie gave the girl a baleful look, then she shrugged as if to say, 'what's done, is done.'

"With Bear! He was under Bear's protection and you had the audacity to use him for the hunt!" cried Mother in a mixture of surprise and anger. "This is really the limit, Grannie. Now we may have real trouble!"

"I'm sure you'll be able to settle it," Grannie grinned with a toothless crooked mouth, and Mother gave her a look saying, 'Oh, shut up!'

She then turned to the girl, "Nimmi, you go and catch us something to eat, a real animal this time but make it good. Don't forget we are having a guest tonight."

As Nimmi turned to go, Finbar looked after her as she vanished, her golden-green leafy cover mingling with the leaves of the trees. The Witch lifted her withered arms, and without much ceremony

Finbar felt again the web covering his body, going through the same process backward until he was standing before the two women in his true human form, amazed to find his clothes on. Suddenly, he felt the sharp pain in his backside; turning to look, he saw the red spot that had spread on his pants.

"You're hurt!" Mother said. "Is it painful?"

"I'll live," he replied with clenched teeth.

"Don't worry, we have the means to cure as much as to hurt. Come now, let's all go home."

She turned to go among the trees, walking in a quick, sure pace as they were bending, clearing the way before her, with Grannie skipping right behind. Finbar followed through a path that had been clear behind the women, noticing that it was a fancy affair, a mixture of reddish-brown and dark gray, as the characteristics of them both. It vanished behind the Minstrel as soon as he passed through, the trees and shrubs joining back together as before.

After walking for some time, they arrived at a clearing, which was larger than any the Minstrel had seen in the forest. Finbar could see nothing beside the forest's undergrowth, which had been smoothed out for convenience; but not the slightest cover except branches from the surrounding trees, nor any sort of furniture except a couple of rocks protruding out of the ground, on which he supposed one could sit with not much comfort. It was not exactly his idea of "home", to come to after a day's traveling or working.

"Here," Mother said, "why don't you lie down and I'll have a look at your wound." She waved her hand and to his astonished eyes a carpet was spread over the ground, and some cushions scattered on it.

As she was tending to his wound, he said, "You haven't asked me about myself at all. Aren't you curious to know?"

"All in good time," she said, comfortably. Her manner was so free and easy and never let him feel awkward about showing her his naked backside.

"You can rest now from your day's adventure and feel yourself at home while we see about dinner," she said when she finished cleaning the wound with some water she brought out of nowhere and smeared it with ointment she produced from an invisible vessel.

As he was able to sit properly at last, he looked up at her and for the first time noticed her greenish-brown eyes. On an impulse, he said, "Your eyes are exactly like Bear's! Are you related in any way?"

To his own ears it sounded an absurd question, but Mother just laughed and replied, "Of course, he is my brother."

Full of questions without answers, the Minstrel lay among the cushions. Looking up at Mother, he saw her moving her arms and getting some stones to arrange themselves in a circle, and a flip of her hand created fire to burn in its center. The two women were moving about in their preparation and soon the Minstrel felt too weary to follow their action. At last he closed his eyes and slept.

• • •

When Finbar opened his eyes again, night had fallen and the only light illuminating the clearing came from the fire in its center. Finbar could smell the aroma of cooking, stirring the saliva in his mouth and a gargling in his empty stomach.

"Hey, stranger," he saw Nimmi standing and calling to him, "come and join us. And don't worry, I won't chase you again!" Her voice was as clear as gold and her laughter rolled like glass beads on a hard floor. He rose and approached the fire.

Mother, who was standing over it, said, "There is a stream of water running just at the edge of the clearing. As you go and wash, dinner will be ready."

When he came back, feeling refreshed and alive again, she said, "Now is the time to tell us about yourself. We can't eat together with one who is a stranger."

Settling down in front of some leafy dishes full of all kinds of food, Finbar said, "My name is Finbar and I'm a minstrel."

"Haven't I heard about you somewhere?" croaked the old woman. Finbar could see that she appeared now more as a grandmother than a witch, finding it easier to talk to her. "That's why you were with Bear and it was showing you our forest, wasn't it?"

"But why did you want to hunt and eat me?" Finbar asked.

"We didn't know it at the time, of course!" she retorted.

"Oh Grannie, what have we done?" Nimmi laughed in chastising the old woman.

"You can see, now, Grannie, how right I was!" Mother added. "Can you imagine the tales his spirit would have spread about us if you'd had your way!"

"Forget it!" the old one croaked. What's done is done, and he is alive and well among us. Let's eat and tell stories afterwards!"

It was the first time for Finbar to eat sitting on the ground and eating with his fingers, because that was how things were done in the forest. But he enjoyed his food no less, or perhaps even more than sitting on a proper chair at a proper table. The meal was delicious, being as fresh as it was; instead of lamps, torches, or candles they had the stars twinkling at them from the clear sky, and the forests mysterious night sounds served as music. The Minstrel learned much about the exploits of the three women in the forest, realizing them to be as old as the forest itself and as powerful. He could almost give them a mythological name but decided to leave their mystery alone for the time being.

When the last crumb of food vanished from the table, Nimmi said to Finbar, "Let's play by the brook; it's very nice there at this time of night."

He rose without a question and they walked over to where it flowed, burbling softly among some fallen leaves and soft undergrowth.

A silver glow rested on the face of the water, flickering on the ripple like myriad stars. Nimmi stepped in it and sat in the water, her leafy cover dissolved off her body. Her bare skin shone greenish-gold, flickering on the silver water. "Come on and join me," she whispered.

Finbar shed his clothes, deciding it was ridiculous to be ashamed before such innocence. He stepped in a little carefully, for the stream's bottom was covered with pebbles. Nimmi stretched her arm and tripped him, and he fell face down in the water right beside her. She started sprinkling him, caressing his body with her wet hands, and he felt and saw his arousal, unable to stop himself. She started playing with his body, and soon he found himself, willy-nilly, taking part in her game, thinking at the same time that she was rather young for that kind of play. She showed, though, no sign of being inexperienced, and soon they were involved together, bodies intertwined, caressing and nibbling and holding fast and then penetrating. It was an exhilarating game, and he came a few times. When they were spent at last, she stood up and pulled him to his feet. As soon as they came out of the water, her body was covered again with those greenish-gold leaves and then she was gone.

Having put his own clothes on his wet body, Finbar came up to the fire, which was now just some glowing embers. No one was there so the Minstrel lay on the ground and very soon was asleep, too tired to think about the events of the day.

• • •

When he woke up, the sun was peeping from behind the tree-tops. Mother was standing over him, gazing down at him. As Finbar rose from the ground and stood before her, he noticed a change in her body. "Why!" he exclaimed, "you're pregnant!"

She smiled, and a glowing light saturating her face. "Of course, that's what happened when you sleep with a woman."

"But I slept with your daughter, not with you!" he cried out.

"It's all the same," she assured him.

"But how? Why?"

"It's very simple," she replied, swirling her regal dress. "You could not sleep with me because I am Mother, and Nimmi cannot get pregnant because she is too young. D'you see?"

"And you rear your children here, in the forest?"

"They belong in the forest, silly, all my children. I'll have some little piglets from you, who will grow to be nice boars, perhaps with a bit of inspiration inherited from the Minstrel."

Finbar, shocked silent, shook his head, having no words to utter. "Here's your sack," she handed it over to him, "we've put a few things in it for you, so you'll be well provided for on your way."

"But how do I get out of the forest?" he asked. His throat constricted in his agitation and his voice came out hoarse. He calmed himself, cleared his throat and asked, "What direction should I take?"

"Bear will take you to where you were going the first time." As she was talking, Bear appeared from among the trees, a wide grin spread over his bulky face.

"I'm glad to meet you again, Finbar, and that you are safe and sound. It was good of my sister to take care of you as she did." While he was talking in his growling voice, the Minstrel barely notice that Mother had disappeared as the other two women had. They turned to go, but this time the forest did not assume its ghostly form; but, as they did the day before, trees and shrubs cleared the way for the two of them now.

Soon, they arrived at the other end of the forest, and a vista of rolling green hills dotted with small farm houses opened before the Minstrel's eyes. He would certainly have enough audience for the next few days for his new tales and songs he was going to make, about the lovely Nimmi, the beautiful Mother, the horrible Witch Grannie and the kind Bear, who had taught him something about the ancient ways of the forest.

• • •

# THE WATER NYMPH

## I

It was a hot summer day, the land bare with no shade. Finbar the Minstrel had been walking since morning, and when noontime approached, he felt the need for rest. He stopped and looked around him. He had been told at the village where he had stayed the night before that the way he was going led to a river, and he was looking forward to reaching it. Pausing for a minute, he dropped his bag, raised his head and sniffed the air. Had there been any breath of air blowing from the direction of the river, he would have been able to sense its moisture; but throughout the morning no wind blew, and he began losing hope of ever reaching the river. Finbar stood, deep in thoughts. If only he could control the wind – to raise it when needed, like now, or to calm it down when it blew too hard! As if his thoughts affected the air, a light breeze stirred, barely felt, and he turned his face toward it. It caressed his face and dried the sweat on his skin, and then he sensed that trace of moisture he was hoping for and knew the direction he should go.

On his way to the river, Finbar went back in his thoughts to what had happened last night at the village. He stayed there less than a day, having arrived late after noon. He found a place to eat, where he lingered, idly talking to other customers. Soon they found out his occupation, inviting him to present his stock of tales and songs at the village's central fire on the Common that evening. Being too tired to make proper preparation for entertaining his audience, he asked them to make their own choice. There was no agreement among the villagers: the young men wanted to hear tales about wandering knights and their horses, their armor and heroics. The girls wanted romantic songs of love; the old women wanted to hear about witches, dwelling in the forest and practicing their magic; the old men preferred proverbs of wisdom. Finbar, though, for reason of his own, did not listen to any of these requests; his tired mind rejected all suggestions until he heard the voice of one youngish woman saying, "Why don't you tell us about water nymphs who charm men and drown them in rivers or ponds."

A burst of laughter erupted among the villagers. "Ha, Sarina," the men cried from all sides, "you don't need water to charm men and drown them in your bosom!" and the women giggled among themselves in agreement.

Finbar raised his eyes to look at the woman. She had stood up among the sitting people – tall and full of figure though not fat, her body curved in the right places. Her face was well chiseled, with high cheekbones that enhanced her large, lively eyes, their color shining the blue-green of water. Her nose was straight and her mouth full, ready to kiss and be kissed.

The Minstrel smiled at her, weariness miraculously dropping from his body, as if he was drawing liveliness from the woman called Sarina. "I do know a few tales and songs about water nymphs," he said; "d'you want to hear a happy ending or a tragedy."

"If you ask," a middle-aged man burst out, "she would prefer a tragedy – it adds flavor to her sense of power."

"You shut up, Mundy, your tragedy didn't stretch beyond making a fool of yourself," Sarina teased him. "No, Minstrel," she turned to Finbar, "I do like a happy ending, or at least, a beautiful ending even if it is sad."

That evening Finbar accommodated her, singing the sad song of a girl abandoned by her lover, who jumped into the river, drowned and turned into a water nymph; she attracted men with her sad song, pulled them into the river and made them drown. When he finished the song, he let the villagers know that he was too weary to present another. He was then invited to stay the night, having a bed made for him by the Mistress of the house that stood at a corner of the yard; he slept deeply till morning, not even dreaming about Sarina and her desirable body.

# II

The memory of that incident now stirred in Finbar a desire to reach the river quickly. He widened his steps, and soon caught the flicker of gold reflected from water under the sun. In a few moments he was standing on the river's bank, watching the water flowing lazily over the flat bottom. Without much delay Finbar stripped of his clothes and waded in, advancing until he could lift his feet and swim without touching the riverbed. He dipped his head in the water, worked with his arms, turned on his back and blinked at the shining sun. Blinded, he turned on his stomach again, floated on the water with his face dipped in it; again he swam a little and stopped, stretched his arms wide and floated; again he dipped his head and closed his eyes, giving himself in to the refreshing effect of the current.

When he opened them again, something was caught in the corner of his eye. A movement, which was not the waves, interfering with their slight sway. 'A fish,' he thought, 'fine, I'll have something fresh to eat.' He swam toward the shore to get the small net he kept for that purpose. As he stood up in the shallows, something took hold of his ankle. He shook his leg to get it loose, but the hold strengthened. He bent to take a better look at the water, which churned and frothed around him, hiding what was in it. 'A strange fish,' the Minstrel reflected, 'instead of escaping it comes out to be caught.' But the thing did not look like a fish. His leg seemed to be held by human hands!

He bent again and put his hands in the water, trying to catch whatever it was. A long, sleek body with no scales twisted and slipped out of his hands, at the same time releasing his leg. The Minstrel sunk in the water, dipped his head in with open eyes and looked around him. A golden body swam around him in circles, smooth as an eel but glowing in the sunshine, with blue-green hair crowning its head. A woman? He had never seen anything like her, but she looked very much like the water nymph of his stories.

'So,' he murmured, 'you want to play? Let's play, then!' He returned to his swimming, but she leaped ahead of him. He came after her and she turned toward him, jumping above his head out of the water, pulling at his hand and turning him toward her. Then she slipped away again and went back to her circling, and he came after her again. He tried to meet her face to face, but she was too quick for him, slipping away and returning, crushing into his body and getting away... He could not take hold of her, or stop her in her rapid motion. At last he got tired of this frustrating game; he swam to shore and got out of the water. He stood on the bank, erect and nude, his maleness quivering at the thought of caressing the nymph's hair as the water had done, taking hold of her small, firm breasts, twisting his legs with hers...

Indeed, she had legs – not a fish's tale as in the legends. She was a real woman, young to look at, desirable as fresh water on a hot day. She stopped her pranks, then, stood up and faced him, her face smiling and her eyes glittering, grinning at him.

"Come!" Finbar called out to her, "step to the shore and let's see who wins outside the water!"

She shook her head, her hair flowing around it like water, glittering with golden flakes in its blue-green watery color. She said nothing, only lifted her arm and signed to him to come back into the river. He stood there, hesitating, recalling his own tales about those water nymphs, who drew their lovers to drown in the river. Was she able to do it to him? She did not look very strong. But his blood stormed in his veins, the cool water only inflaming his desire.

Slowly, she drew him to her with the beckoning movement of her hand. He advanced back into the river, going step by step through the shallows. The water reached his ankles, touched his calves and knees. He crouched in it, his hand playing with it, and the woman came nearer; he stretched his hand and touched her skin, and it felt like touching flowing water. This nontouch stirred him even more than any woman's touch he had ever experienced. He swam toward her and she stretched her arms, which interlaced with his. She drew him into deeper water, and as his legs stretched to swim, she swam by his side with her legs entwining with his, exactly as he had imagined.

There was nothing to stop him now. As their bodies interlaced together, he entered hers as if flowing with the water. They were now one body with the water, circling and twisting with the waves. He did not exactly lose his consciousness, but his mind fogged and connected with his body and the water. Time itself fragmented and scattered in the fog and he lost all sense, years seemed to pass until his mind cleared again and he felt the chill of the water. He found himself floating alone, his eyes blinded by the westerly sun.

## III

Finbar swam to shore and climbed out of the river, shook his body and lay on the bank naked, drying in the sun. He fell asleep and slept till evening, waking up hungry, not thinking of the river maiden. Putting on his shirt and pants, he took his small fishing net and walked into the shallows. After a little time he caught a nice-size fish, drawing it out from among the stirring waves. He took out his knife and cleaned the fish, gathered some stones in a circle, found some dry sticks and built and lit a fire; in it he put some loose, clean stones, on which he roasted the fish. From his bag he took out a loaf of bread given to him by the Mistress of the house where he had slept the night before. That evening he had a filling and tasty meal.

Twilight time cooled the heat of the day. Finbar sat for a long while on the river bank, watching the breathing wavelets stretching on the water, pondering the day's adventure. Who was the girl who swept his body into such stirring and satisfying, the like of which he had never known before? Was she the same water nymph, about which it was said that she drowned her victims in the river? Evidently, she did not drown him. Was he going to see her again? A sense of yearning rose inside him. She did not seem like any other woman he had ever known – those village women, young and not so young, who would sometimes find their way at night into his temporary bed… More than one individual woman, she seemed to be an ideal of all women, one you can only experience in your wet dreams…

• • •

Darkness fell. Finbar stretched on his back on the ground, his face toward the sky. It was a clear and chilly night. The stars were scattered above his head, glittering cold, and he began telling himself stories about them, about the constellations and the mythological figures they represented. At last his eyes tired and he closed them, falling asleep on the bare ground as he had done many times in his wanderings.

Finbar dreamed, and in his dream he was back in the water, lying under a clear, sunless sky. The Water Nymph was there too; they were not making love but lying on their backs, swaying as in a cradle on the light ripple. She was talking to him, and her voice was like the murmur of the water.

She seemed to be answering his unasked question, "They always drown in the middle of our lovemaking, before I have a chance to talk to them," she murmured softly.

"Why didn't I drown, then?" he wondered.

"I don't really know," she replied. "You must have some special watery talent…"

He paused, then whispered, "I've never met a watery creature like you."

"Ah," she said, "not everyone can…"

They fell silent, the breeze blowing softly over the ripple. He shivered, but it was a pleasant sensation. After a while, he asked, "Why do you drown them?"

"I don't," she protested, softly. "In their excitement, their souls leave their bodies, floating astray on the water. Then they lose their bearings and don't know how to come back, before they sink into the water and drown…"

"Enchanted…" Finbar murmured, recalling his own feeling. "But he did go back, being too – " he was unable to define it, and in his confusion the dream dissolved into utter darkness, and he slept soundly till morning.

# IV

Finbar woke blinded by sunrays, which penetrated through his eyelids. He breathed in deeply before opening his eyes, then stretched his arms sideways, as if trying to swim again. He was not being cradled by the water, though, but lying on hard ground. Something stirred in his heart, the memory of something beautiful, glowing but so slippery that he was unable to grasp it, lost it both from his hands and from his mind.

He rose to his feet and went down to the river, where he had a drink of water and washed his face. There was no sign of anything alive in the river, and he turned to pick up his belongings, put everything in his bag and threw it over his shoulder. Looking around him, he noticed some wooded hills and decided to go in that direction; it would be a good change from the flat, dull, hot country he had been walking in for too long a time.

• • •

# WINTER ON THE MOUNTAIN

## I

As Finbar was walking along the mountain foot from one village to the next, it started raining, and the Minstrel found shelter for the night in a shallow cave. The mountain slope was high and steep, and the Minstrel was able to see the glare of snow on its top, although down below the winter was relatively mild. He had no intention of climbing to the top, where he would find no audience for his bagful of songs and tales as he did on the plains and the low hills; he was happy to be able to lie under the rough roof of the cave on dry ground, close his eyes and sleep in peace.

He woke early the next morning, expecting nothing in particular except continuing on his way; Finbar was ready to do it even if it was still raining, having a good refreshing night's sleep. He rose on his feet, took a sip of water from his bottle and washed his face, put on his coat and picked up his bag, ready to continue on his way. Stopping at the entrance to the cave, the Minstrel saw that although the sun was hidden behind a thick blanket of clouds, the rain had stopped for the time being, and he hoped he could do a good bit of walking toward the nearest village without getting wet.

As he was coming out of the cave, though, a large bird was blocking his way. It was an eagle, but he had never seen such a large one before. It was flapping its enormous wings and, to the Minstrel's astonishment, it started talking.

"Good morning, Finbar. I trust you had a good night sleep and are ready for your new adventure."

"Oh!" For a moment, Finbar was unable to utter more than that. Then, mustering a little courage, he asked, "Who are you and what do you want with me?"

The eagle stretched up to its full height, which was still far less than a human's size, and said, "I am the queen of this mountain, and you're invited to spend some time in my realm at its peak."

"Oh – eh –" the Minstrel hesitated. "I'm sorry – I think – I'm due somewhere – "

"Don't talk nonsense, Finbar. You're not going to miss out on an adventure for nothing, are you?"

Indeed, to this Finbar had no answer except ask, "But how am I to reach the peak of the mountain? I am not sure I can climb this cliff."

"Don't worry about that, I'm going to take you up there on my back."

"Your back? It doesn't look –" But before the Minstrel finished his sentence, he saw the eagle begin to stretch up and sideways, grow and grow until it was no smaller than a horse. It spread now huge wings and said with an authoritative voice, "Come, now, climb on my back and we shall go!"

There was nothing more for Finbar to say or do so he did as he was told. The eagle's back was no less comfortable than that of a horse; it flapped its wings once and twice and soon was up in the air. It was the kind of trip that Finbar had never taken before; unfortunately, the day was still cloudy and the valley was covered with thick fog; the only sight the Minstrel was able to see was that of the mountain with its steep slope, against which they were now rising upward. Finbar sensed that they were going very close to the clouds themselves.

At last, the flight was over; they reached the peak, the eagle landed and the Minstrel alighted from its back; as he did so, his feet sunk in piles of fresh snow, that continued to fall around them. The bird then changed its shape right before his eyes, becoming what it had claimed to be: the Queen of the Mountain. She was very tall, much taller than Finbar himself. She had a snow white face, and her shiny black hair fell straight below her shoulders; her eyes were like a pair of black holes. She was clad in a long black dress that reached the snowy ground, and it was spread with tiny white dots that sparkled like the snow that covered the ground.

"Goodbye, Minstrel," the Queen said then; "but I think we might meet again." With these words, she shrunk back into the size and figure of an eagle; it spread its wings and flew away, leaving the Minstrel amazed, wondering what he was going to do, and not a little alarmed by his sudden solitude.

Because the snowy mountain peak was nothing like the earth below. Nothing grew up here, there were no little animals rushing about and no birds flying in the sky that was not seen at all for the clouds. Finbar felt a chill that penetrated through his clothes that froze not only his body but even his mind; he was unable to think what he might do now. To his amazement, although the trip had started in the morning and was not very long, it now looked as if evening was falling; soon, he felt, dark night will come, and he would be even more lost than now. The snow had become heavier, and he felt he should look for some shelter, otherwise he might freeze to death with no one to help him.

· · ·

The Minstrel started walking, not knowing where he was going. After a while, he noticed a rock jutting out of the ground, giving a kind of half shelter under it. At least, it was free of the falling snow, so he crouched there, tightened his coat around him, and tried to close his eyes against this hostile world he had found himself in.

Night had fallen, and the Minstrel lay in the dark, listening to the silence. It was eerie but peaceful, however full of expectation. The wind rose and broke the silence, and in the wind he could hear other sounds. These were like the howling of some animals, and Finbar thought they might be jackals. Normally, he was not afraid of jackals; they were small animals and as a rule, did not attack humans. But this howl was unsettling, making the Minstrel's imagination work too hard; in his mind eyes he began seeing such unpleasant pictures that could not be driven away even when you close your eyes.

The howling increased, came closer and closer. The Minstrel's heart fluttered, his fright became almost unbearable. He was ready to rise and leave his shelter, to run away for his life, when he saw numerous shiny dots sparkling through the darkness – exactly like the shiny dots on the Queen's black dress. Finbar froze in his place. The dots came in pairs, and he realized they were eyes, shining white in the beasts' black heads; soon they came close enough so he could discern the vague shapes of the animals they belonged to. And now, right below the pairs of eyes, he was able to see white, sharp teeth inside the gaping black mouths. His own teeth chattered, his limbs shook violently, and he just sat in his place, waiting for the most horrible thing to happen.

• • •

Even the Minstrel's imagination, though strong, was not enough to make him understand the horror he was destined to go through on that night. In a fit of daring, one of the beasts burst forward and snapped its teeth at Finbar. Soon the others accompanied it, snapping and biting at his clothes, dragging him out into the open. They were in such great number that he was certain he could never stand against their attack. The only thing he could think of was trying to run away, and this he did.

Still, they came after him. There seemed to be droves of them, filling the whole space around him, creating a mosaic of black and white, swarming over him. They were getting wilder and wilder, dancing around him, jumping and leaping all over him. One animal jumped so high it landed on Finbar's shoulder, and a sharp pain ran through his cheek as the jackal bit it. The warm feeling of blood mingled with the cold moisture of the snow on Finbar's face, the pain as sharp as the cold biting at his nerves, making him tremble as he saw red drops falling, coloring the white ground. The sight of blood excited the animals even more and, they pulled his clothes away, they were getting a clear access to his body. One beast leaped on top of his head, threw off his hat and started pulling at his hair and his scalp. Finbar, completely helpless, was ready to drop.

A new sound appeared above that of the wind and the jackals, shrieking in a harsh, half-human voice, "Kill him! Spill his blood!"

Then he saw her again, the Queen of the Mountain. She was dancing with the storm and with the snow, creating another fantasy in black and white; in a bizarre moment he thought he might have enjoyed the sight if he was not so full of pain and terror. She screamed, repeating again and again, "Kill him! Spill his red blood on the white snow! Let us have our sacrifice of Midwinter!"

So, that was it, the Minstrel thought while running and skipping and stumbling and falling and rising again to resume his running. He was to be a winter sacrificial victim, as appeared in many of his tales. He was part of one of his tales, and there was nothing he could do about it. He did not know where to run, which way to escape, so he ran blindly into the falling snow, his feet sinking into the soft blanket piling up. He pulled his feet out and continued to run, with the animals chasing him, hanging on to the tatters of his clothes, clinging to his badly bitten body. In the cold and the fright he stopped feeling the pain, but there was a limit to how far he could run. At last, he fell and was unable to rise again, and the jackals were on top of him instantly, jumping on his prostrate body, tearing up at his flesh, with the figure of the Queen looming over them with her urgent cries for sacrifice.

As Finbar's red blood sprinkled on the white snow under the jackals' black heads, he thought again, 'Am I going to die here, a Midwinter sacrifice? Is there no salvation for me?' But his thoughts got more and more confused, as his mind blurred and his body relaxed at last into a deep faint.

• • •

He stirred into stillness, as the wind had calmed down and the beasts vanished together with their Queen. Finbar raised his head from the pile of snow he was buried in; the place was a desert of white snow with no sign of life. He stumbled out, shook away the snow and tried to walk. The ground was rough, but he continued, insistent, advancing in an unknown direction. Just not to stay put, just to feel himself alive and moving, no matter how and where.

Then he saw the Queen again, a silent black figure on the white snow. She was standing still amidst the still forms of the jackals; her arm was raised above her head, with its white face and black hair, and in her hand there was a shining knife. Finbar froze again, shocked to see the knife, knowing it was directed at his heart. He jumped. Not ready to be a lamb brought to slaughter, he started running again, not knowing whether they were running after him or not. Then he stumbled on a rock and fell, and before he knew what was happening, he was rolling down the slope of the mountain.

Down and down he rolled, with the snow gathering on top and around his body; like a snowball he rolled down the hill, on and on, endlessly. He lost consciousness again, rolling down the slope of the mountain wrapped around with the accumulating snow, spinning like a giant wheel. It stopped at last, having reached rock bottom. There the pile lay still, with the man inside it stunned, unconscious.

• • •

Finbar woke up, back in the shallow cave he had gone to sleep in. For a moment still wrapped in his fright, he was blinded by bright light hitting his eyes. At first, he thought this was the whiteness of the snow; then his mind cleared and he realized it was the sun shining outside. He rose and stretched, then walked slowly, pondering, toward the entrance of the cave.

Under clear blue sky and bright sunlight, the ground was covered with fresh, green grass, with colorful flowers scattered everywhere in all their glory.

"Hey, Minstrel," he heard a young, clear voice ringing out, "and how do you feel this morning?"

With a fluttering heart, recalling the dread of last night, the Minstrel raised his eyes to meet a wonderful vision. It was a very different female apparition from that of last night. She was young and trim and very pretty. Although her hair was black, it was curved in shiny curls; her black eyes sparkled with laughter; and the cheeks on her pale face blossomed like roses; her lips were blood red and she was smiling at him, her voice ringing like a sweet bell.

"Midwinter is over, Finbar, so you can forget my wicked sister and her exploits," she said. "It's spring morning now, so you should be happy again."

"I can't say I quite understand what was happening," Finbar said, weakly.

"It's not always necessary to understand, as long as you tell a good story," she declared. "But you should be all right now, and can continue on your way in peace."

He had more questions to ask, but she did not wait for him. Right before his eyes she seemed to melt away, mingling with the colorful flowers of the green meadow. But she left behind her that new sense of well being and cheerfulness that enabled him at last to take to the road again, looking for the next village where he could stop among human beings and present them with his ware of songs and tales.

• • •

# DRAGON RIDE

## I

Finbar the Minstrel was not happy. The day was bleak, and he knew he should have stayed behind in the village where he had been visiting, had the people there been more hospitable and forthcoming. They usually welcomed him as a good natured stranger who had come to entertain them with his songs and tales, and teach them something of the ways of the world. But in that village, whose name he did not even remember, for some reason unknown to him they were all sour-faced and grumpy, had no patience for him or his lore; they allowed him to sleep the night in a stable, rather than invite him into one of their homes. He rose early, and without any break-fast – which would usually be served to him by a kind hostess – he threw his bag over his shoulder and left without saying goodbye to anyone.

The sky was heavy with clouds and he had to wear his coat, but he preferred the hardship of Nature to that of humanity. Toward noon the rain started falling, first in hesitating drops, then in torrents. Tightening his hat on his head and wrapping his coat around his body, the Minstrel peeped around, looking for shelter. There were some low hills at a distance, and he set his steps in that direction, feeling that was better than staying in the open field where he had been walking.

It was a longer walk than he had estimated, but at last he reached the foothills. Closer up, the hills looked higher than he thought when seen from the distance, and some cliffs looming above his head indicated the possibility of the existence of some niches he could use for shelter. Indeed, Finbar's luck changed at that point, when he spotted a dark opening that could be the entrance to a cave. Without hesitation, he hurried toward the place, passed through the opening and found himself inside a spacious cavern; he threw his bag to the ground, removed his drenched coat and hat and shook himself all over like a wet dog.

What he did not notice at first was that the cave was occupied. A deep growl soon put him wise to the fact, and when he turned to look toward the depth of the cave, he encountered a pair of gleaming yellow eyes, that could only belong to some wild animal. Finding himself in such straights, between the torrential rain outside and a possible preying animal inside, Finbar stood glued to his place, his heart beating hard and his whole body shaking. He never thought himself a hero, but such fear that had taken hold of him now was rare even for him.

A new indication of danger appeared in the form of a roaring sound from the entrance of the cave. Turning to look, Finbar's heart turned stopped momentarily, and he felt death was coming in person to fetch him. What he saw was no less threatening than what he heard. An enormous body blocked the cave's opening, its strange silhouette appearing on the background of the day's faint light. The scaly head of the beast hinted at just one thing: a Dragon! Even the mysterious animal in the depth of the cave retreated before that giant.

"Now, now, Finbar," a deep, low growl sounded, hinting at an effort to be gentle and calm. Suddenly the blood rushed throughout the Minstrel's limbs and his numbed heart beat like mad. A talking dragon? Would that be the same Dragon Lady that once saved him from some alarming soldiers?

"Yes, Finbar," the Dragon roared as if in answer to the Minstrel's thoughts; "you know I'm not going to eat you. I need your help."

Slowly, hesitatingly, Finbar picked up his bag, put his coat back on and wrapped it tight around his body as wet as it still was, and went toward the cave's entrance. The Dragon moved away, allowing him to come out. The rain, the Minstrel noticed, had stopped, and the sun peeped out from among the still heavy clouds. The Dragon's coppery scales glimmered in the sunlight like gold.

"Are you ready to climb on my back and take off? We have to hurry," claimed the Dragon.

"Take off where? And why? What can I do to help you?" asked the Minstrel with some suspicion.

"I can't tell you much, except that we are going to save a princess," the Dragon replied, a little impatient.

"To save a princess! From what? You know I'm not a hero, Lady!"

"I know that," answered the Dragon, looking pitifully at Finbar. "I am not sure why you have been chosen for the task, but there you are, and I don't see how you can get away from it. So, come on, get on with it."

Finbar reflected. To ride a Dragon! Indeed, that could be quite an experience, and a good subject to tell his audience – if he comes out alive from such a feat! "Why don't you tell me first about that princess, and why does she need to be saved, won't you?" he pleaded.

"Well, I suppose that's just right, and I don't think too much time will be lost by it," the Dragon lady agreed, as if relenting her cross attitude. "She's been a prisoner for such a long time that a few more minutes will not make much difference."

"A long time? How long? Are you telling me a fairy tale?" Finbar asked, suspicion creeping back into his heart, thinking the whole thing might be a hoax.

"Well..." The Dragon was clearly hesitating before resuming the story. "Look, Finbar, first, it's not a hoax, the princess really exists. And second, I'm not sure about the time schedule, but I know she needs saving, so I think you should come, anyway, see?"

"Well, if you put it like that... Just tell me what she needs saving from, and then I'll be sure to climb on your back – though I'm not so sure how – and come with you, all right?"

"All right, then. The princess, whose name is Mayka, has been taken prisoner by some highwaymen, a long time ago, as I said, and never heard from since, until just lately, when some of the forest's braver creatures brought word of the place she had been hidden at, and it was decided that an attempt at saving her should take place. Again, why you were chosen for this job I cannot tell, but I was sent to bring you, as the quickest way to do it."

"Very well, then," the Minstrel said. "Now, how do I climb onto your back?"

In the best of story tradition, the Dragon bent a leg, on which Finbar stepped and, given a boost, was pushed onto the Dragon's back. As he was settling down among the scales, he found his seat extremely uncomfortable, but said nothing, as he had made his decision and was going to bide by it.

# II

The flight was uneventful and, having got used to it in a short time, the Minstrel began to enjoy it, particularly the opportunity to look at the earth from above. All these fields and hills, mountains and rivers, which he had been used to seeing at close quarters, appeared now as a shapely mosaic of forms and colors. Indeed, here was something to tell his audience of his own experience, not what he had heard and read from other sources.

At high noon they arrived at their destination, which was a strange meeting place between a wide desert and a thick forest. Finbar wondered at such a place, and the contradictions it would create, by force. Peeping down from the Dragon's back, the Minstrel could see various shapes of beings scattered around, wandering between those two sorts of habitats as if not sure where they belonged. Finbar was thinking that perhaps, they belonged to none of those, having come from distant places so different that nothing local was familiar to them.

Such thoughts seemed quite probable when ascribed to the creatures, among which the Dragon lady now landed. It came down right by the side of a great strange figure that seemed attached to a large rock. As Finbar alighted, he looked in amazement at that shape that stood in the middle of all the other strange shapes that filled the area. That must be a Sphinx, he told himself.

According to his knowledge of old myths, it was made of the stone it was crouching on, actually forming a part of it. It had the shapely head of a woman and rounded bare breasts; its crouching body was that of a lion, with lion's paws underneath it; and the restless tail attached to its backside had the head of a snake at its end. A pair of folded eagle's wings grew on the creature's back and, as Finbar approached the crouching figure, they spread out while the tail rose to the air and the snake's head hissed at him.

At that moment the Dragon turned itself into its alternative figure of a beautiful lady and said, "Meet my sister, the Sphinx, Finbar."

With a fluttering heart Finbar came up to the Sphinx. He could see the kindness in its large, brown eyes, and in spite of the hissing snake, the woman's head spoke gently to him in an obviously female voice. "Come on, Finbar," she said, "you don't need to be afraid of me, you know! I'm always ready to hear some of your songs and tales, which amuse me enormously, though we don't have time for it now, but perhaps later, when all this is over."

The Minstrel approached the Sphinx and bent his head before her. "Your Highness, I'm so honored to meet you!" He fell silent, not knowing how to go on, how to ask about his intended mission.

"You want to hear all about your mission, I know, and why you were chosen for it," she said. "Let me first introduce to you some of my company, though they are too many for you to know them all," she said, then called out, "Children, come and meet Finbar the Minstrel, and learn how we can all together help to save our Princess!"

Some of the strange beings came closer, others seemed too shy to approach. Finbar thought he should have known most of the ones he saw closely, like the Chimera, who was the Sphinx's relative; Pegasus, the winged horse, (and Finbar wondered why he was not the one sent for him instead of the Dragon); a pair of Centaurs and a couple of Babylonian demons. He did not recognize Quetzalcoatl, the Aztec winged snake, when the Sphinx presented him; but he was quite familiar with the figure of Lilit as a beautiful young woman, with her owl's wings and claws.

"I'll tell you the problem now, and why we cannot get at Princess Mayka without your help," the Sphinx said. "You see, some evil men put her in the midst of that forest, under a heavy guard of vicious beasts, for the purpose of being worshiped as their goddess. Unfortunately, they had not asked Princess Mayka's permission, or even if she wished to be their Goddess, and these things cannot be allowed. We have found all that out only a short time ago when Mother Bear came back to her own forest after a long trip through her many domains around the world. Mother Bear found the Princess, of whose existence she had had no knowledge, guarded and looked after by a mixed bunch of beastly animals, which it was beyond her power to fight on her own. She then applied to me for help, knowing I had the rule over a great many creatures with all kinds of wonderful abilities."

Finbar listened very attentively to the story, and when the Sphinx paused, he said, "I still don't see what I can do in the matter. You certainly have amassed a bunch of very able creatures, who must be better qualified than me to perform such a feat."

"My creatures," replied the Sphinx, "have one tendency, which you lack, and that is viciousness and blood shedding. This is not what I want. I much prefer to use your knack of talking and gentle persuasion."

"You want me to work to release the Princess from her vicious guard without bloodshed?" asked Finbar, not quite believing such a tale.

"Exactly! I am absolutely certain of your ability to fulfill such a task!"

Finbar fell silent. Absentmindedly, he fell to watching the creatures around him, who seemed agitated, rising on their feet, opening their great jaws to show their ferocious teeth while uttering loud roars and flapping their wings, as if ready to help if necessary.

Shaking all over but trying hard to overcome his alarm and fear, Finbar said at last, clearing his voice and shaking his head, "what do you want me to do, then?"

"What I want you to do is charm those vicious, beastly animals with calming words and fascinating music, as you do with human beings," the Sphinx explained, suddenly rising on her lion's feet and stretching her eagle's wings. She was the most magnificent creature Finbar had ever seen, and he actually cowered before her, unintentionally.

"And how do I get close enough to those animals without being devoured myself?" he asked, simply.

"You ride my sister, the Dragon, of course; that's why you need her and not any of the other winged creatures. With her fire she can clear the area around the Princess, while you choose your most suitable songs to sing to them from above."

The plan sounded quite simple, and Finbar understood why he and the Dragon had been chosen for it. There was nothing more to discuss, then; he and the Dragon Lady turned aside to make their plan, then took their rest for the day, so that they would be refreshed in the morning.

# III

The day had risen bright and clear, when the Minstrel rode the Dragon toward the thick forest in order to save the captive princess; below them, Mother Bear ran through the thicket to show them the way. After a long while, when Finbar almost got bored with the endless sight of the thick forest, she stopped and pointed with her snout in a certain direction, signing to them she could go no further. She then turned and left, leaving the two high above to perform their task on their own.

"I think it's up to you, Dragon, to clear some of this dense vegetation, so that we can see what we are doing," said Finbar, holding himself tight while his mount nodded her enormous head. The Dragon took a deep breath, almost unsettling the Minstrel, then she opened her mouth and a long tongue of flame burst out. She circled around the area burning some trees and undergrowth, and then an amazing picture appeared before the Minstrel.

"I think it's enough for now, Dragon," he said quietly, gazing at the sight in wonder.

At the center of the wide clearing that was created in the middle of the dense forest stood a golden throne; on it sat the most beautiful woman the Minstrel had ever seen. She had a lovely face surrounded by golden hair; her shapely body was clad in a long, bright red dress that fell almost to her small feet that were encased in golden sandals, resting on a footrest. On her head she wore a golden crown set with flashing red jewels.

The throne was surrounded by all kinds of beasts that were walking about restlessly; these formed one of the strangest sights Finbar had ever seen. They were not shaped as individual beasts like lions, tigers, wolves or Hyenas; instead, their heads and bodies were mixed together, creating a great confusion of no coherent shape. One thing, though, all these animals had in common: they all showed their ferocious nature by displaying sharp claws and flashing teeth, well prepared to attack any newcomer and filling the Minstrel's heart with great dread.

"It's your turn now, Finbar," the Dragon said; "yours and your songs'."

Slowly, with a quivering voice, the Minstrel started singing an old lullaby that his mother used to sing to him when he was very little. Gradually, the beasts stopped moving about and began to nod, their eyelids fluttered and closed, their bodies dropped to the ground until at last they were all fast asleep.

The Dragon circled once and twice again, to make sure all was quiet down below, then she gradually flew down and landed just in front of the throne. As Finbar alighted, he could not take his eyes off the princess, but then he began to notice what he had not seen before. Looking at her beautiful face, he saw that it was completely lifeless. Her brilliant blue eyes, like a pair of aquamarine jewels, did not notice anything around her; she saw neither the Minstrel nor the Dragon, who were now standing right before her, nor paid any attention to the sleeping beasts; the glazed eyes were staring at something in the distance without moving, without changing. There was no smile on the Princess's face, no sadness or anger, or any other expression. When Finbar looked closely at the golden hair falling from the princess' head, he saw that where it reached her arms it turned into golden ropes that tied the sitting woman to her seat! The ties looked quite tight, and the Minstrel could imagine how hard it would be for her to try and unfasten them, even if she had been awake!

She was indeed a prisoner! Finbar turned to the Dragon, who was standing close beside him. "Now, what do we do?" he whispered his question.

"Now, I think, you should play something to wake her up," the Dragon said with the gentlest growl she could produce.

Nodding his head, the Minstrel put his hand into his bag and produced a small reed flute of his own making. He put it to his lips, and the sweetest jolly tune flowed around the forest clearance. After a while, Finbar saw the golden ropes slacken, getting loose around the princess's arms, turning back into gleaming hair. The princess's eyelids fluttered and, as the blood started flowing through her veins, her white cheeks assumed a rosy color; her lips swelled and parted in a smile, and the life returned to her brilliant blue eyes. There was some confusion in them at first, as she asked in a soft, sweet voice, "What is going on?"

"Princess Mayka," Finbar bowed before her, "we have come to rescue you."

"Rescue? From what? From whom?" The confusion in her eyes grew and spread over her face and her body. She shrunk in her sitting position, as if recoiling from some unknown danger she had not realized until now.

"You have been kidnapped by those beasts," he pointed at them.

"But why?"

"They have made you their goddess, didn't you know?"

"Goddess? Me? You must be joking! I think you've got it all wrong. Who am I to be anyone's goddess?"

The Minstrel looked around him in confusion. But there was no one to answer him, as the beasts were fast asleep and the Dragon shook her head in ignorance.

"But, Princess Mayka..." the Minstrel started again, only to be interrupted.

"Mayka? My name is Jinny! I'm not a princess and I've never been kidnapped?" she cried out.

"There must have been some confusion indeed," said the Minstrel, "because we have found you tied to this golden throne."

"Golden throne? Oh!" Realizing what she was sitting on, the girl jumped out of it and looked around her, full of fright and alarm. "It must have been magic." she whispered.

"What kind of magic?" Finbar asked, very gently, seeing that she was both frightened and confused.

"I remember now; I used to dream... daydreams, you know, not in my sleep... My mother used to scold me for not doing the work properly..." She paused.

"What kind of work?" Finbar asked, glancing at the Dragon, seeking understanding. The Dragon's heavy head swung from side to side, as if not quite understanding such human problems.

The Minstrel resumed his questioning. "What kind of work did your mother said you didn't do properly?" he asked, not quite knowing what kind of work a princess was supposed to do.

"You know," she replied, "like milking the cows, weeding the fields, washing the floors – all the chores done around the house and farm…"

The Minstrel stared, horrified, at the princess, thinking she must be out of her mind. At that moment, though, things had begun to change around that supposedly royal person, as if an enchantment was gradually lifting, either from his eyes or from the place he was at. Instead of the golden throne on which a princess had been sitting a moment ago, there stood now a heap of dry leaves mixed with dirt, surrounded by some flowering shrubs that were still smoldering from the Dragon's burning fire.

While those changes were taking place, the girl continued to tell her story. "You see, I used to go about dreaming instead of working; I think, by some magic act, these dreams came true… One day, right in the middle of feeding the chicken, I was all of a sudden sitting on this golden throne, tied down by my golden hair, and being worshiped by ferocious animals that saw their goddess in me… They wouldn't let me go back home, just bowing and scraping before me as if I was a real princess… For god's sake! Do I look like a real princess?"

As she was uttering those words, Finbar stared at her, full of amazement. Indeed, she no longer looked like any kind of royalty. The girl calling herself Jinny had changed in such an astonishing way. She was pretty enough with her short brown hair and lively hazel eyes; dressed in a light green blouse and a short brown skirt she was still shod with heavy farm boots. The horrifying beast as well had changed, having turned one by one into farm boys who were stirring from sleep all around them.

"Now, Prin – er – Jinny," the Minstrel opened again, "What would you like to do now?"

"I'd like to go home," she said. "I've been so bored sitting here, doing nothing, so I don't mind a little bit of farm work for a change. I think I've had enough of adventure for the time being..." Her voice was soft and pleasant to his ear, though not exactly majestic in tone.

"Would you like to fly the Dragon home, then?" he asked.

"Is this a real Dragon, then? Not a horse pretending to be one, like in my dream?" She was the one to be amazed now, instead of the Minstrel.

"Yes, she is a real Dragon, though not of your world. But you'll have to show us the way to your home village, you know."

"That's all right, I'm sure I can do that from the back of the Dragon."

"And what about these guardians of yours?" he pointed out the lads, who were waking up rubbing their eyes and looking around them with obviously foggy minds.

She laughed, and Finbar realized he liked her laughter, which was gay and free and smiling. "Oh, these scam should be able to take care of themselves! They'll have to get back on foot and it will serve them right for kidnapping me, even if it was magic!"

As they mounted the Dragon and settled on her back, Finbar asked Jinny who had created the magic that had brought her to the forest. "Why, I did, of course!"

After that, she pointed to the Dragon the way she should fly, and then they rode in silence. The Minstrel pondered on that experience of his, which he thought was one of the most wonderful adventures that had happened to him. He was already trying out words and music for the new tale he had to tell a captive audience.

• • •

# THROUGH THE CIRCLE

## I

The Circle appeared before Finbar's eyes unexpectedly. The Minstrel had been walking the whole day in the hot, dry weather. At mid-day, having taken a long draught from his water bottle, he climbed a low hill, and gazed at the wide valley that opened before him on the other side. Green patches promised the possible proximity of water, and he rushed down the hill toward them. He arrived at some tall reeds and, parting them, looked with relief at the small brook that flowed there, hidden among the rushes. He knelt down to drink, sprayed his hot face and filled his bottle, and only then he stood up and looked around him.

The patches of green were bunches of tall reed and high grass, through which flowed that meandering stream, its water sparkling in flushes of blue with dots of gold, reflecting the sun. Finbar then noticed a tall rock standing upright among the green; wondering for a moment at its incongruous appearance, he glanced beyond it and saw that this rock was not the only one. Another upright stone was standing not far from the first, and another and another. It was a whole circle of such tall rocks looming from the flat land of the valley.

The Minstrel pondered that phenomenon for a while. In his extensive traveling, he had heard mention here and there of such stone circles; but, not only had he never seen it with his own eyes, he had also never learned about its purpose or meaning, either from the writings of fables and myths from which he had drawn many of his stories, or from local gossip and anecdotes. Now, as he saw it himself, he thought it was up to him to find out all he could about it.

Slowly, the Minstrel advanced toward the stone closest to him. He was walking in a southern direction, and the sun was glaring in his eyes. There was very little life in the valley, as the season of bird nesting had been long over. He heard no chirping, only some sparrows were flying among the rushes, and a larger bird of prey hovered in the sky; a very light breeze barely touched the reed tops, making them sway like a small ripple, and drying the sweat off the Minstrel's face. Otherwise, the world was almost standing still, waiting for Finbar to act.

Arriving at the northernmost stone of the circle, the Minstrel stopped as the sunrays hit and blinded his eyes. He had just put up his hand to shade them, when a sense of magic touched him from the direction of the circle, and he hesitated before entering it. Was there really something special about such construction, so different from anything he had ever known or seen?

A light cloud passed over the sun, and the Minstrel removed his hand from his eyes. He made a few more paces, reached the stone and touched it lightly; another step and he was inside the circle...

## II

"Here you are," a woman's voice addressed Finbar; "you know we couldn't start without you."

"Start what?" he asked in amazement, and thought, 'Where have all these people come from?'

Indeed, the circle was crowded with people, all dressed in gaudy clothes, shouting words he could not understand. The woman who had spoken to him stood out as if she was their leader; she was tall and majestic, dressed in a mauve color robe and wearing a colorful crown on her dark red hair. "It's time for Midsummer sacrifice, and the prophecy claimed you were going to attend this time."

"Me?"

"Aren't you Finbar the Minstrel? There you are, then, it was you we've been waiting for. Now, take this knife and cut the victim's throat. That will dedicate you to the Goddess, whom you've been worshiping all your life!"

"Indeed, I don't know what you're talking about! Me, cut a victim's throat? I'd rather die myself!"

"Very well, then, he will cut yours, although that was not the occasion we've expected. But there is no difference to me, you know, one of you must die at this hour!"

"No! You can't do that! I'm only here by accident!" the Minstrel cried out. He felt he could never be a hero, only a teller of tales and a singer of songs. Who was he to be a victim at Midsummer?

"Be a hero for once, then, and cut his throat for the good of all! Now! Take that knife in your hand! That's it! Do it, now!"

She was leading him by the hand. He had shut his eyes in alarm, but the woman held his hand tight and led it to the spot. He felt it hit, and a hot gush splashed in his face. Opening his eyes, the whole world had turned red around him. Blinded and feeling faint, Finbar suddenly felt himself all alone in the circle. The celebrants were gone, as were the woman and the victim. He sat down on the ground beside the upright rock, his heart beating fast and his thoughts in a swirl.

## III

Under the hot, midday sun, the Minstrel had fallen asleep. When he woke up, the sun was sinking in the west. Opposite, in the east, a circular full moon appeared; the rays of the setting sun together with those of the rising moon fell on the westernmost stone, crowning it with a soft, golden-silver glow. Finbar rose to his feet and, as if compelled by an unseen force, walked toward that upright rock. The circle was filled with people again, all dressed in gray and black; as he walked through the crowd to reach the westerly stone, they

cleared the way for him. When he reached that stone, he was astonished to see a wide stretch of water open beyond it; he was absolutely
certain there could be no such stretch of water where they were,
nothing that looked more like the sea than a land-bound lake.

"There you are," he heard the same voice again, and the majestic
woman appeared before him, dressed in dark blue with many stars
shining all over her robe. The crown on her head glowed silver, and
she was holding a torch in her hand.

"What is going on here?" he asked, his voice hoarse from worry.
On the water, not far from the shore, a highly decorated boat was
floating, and in it lay the figure of a man.

"What is he doing there?" he asked the woman, than added,
"and who is he, anyway?"

"He is your victim, remember?" she answered, handing out the
torch to him. "Here, you must complete your task, now, and set fire
to the boat."

"Set fire to the body of a man? Are you crazy?"

"He must burn, you know; otherwise, his soul will never reach
heaven?" she insisted. "Here, take it!"

Her voice was as compelling as ever and Finbar felt he had no
choice; he took the torch, but stood there, frustrated, unable to move.

"Come, we'll do it together," she said, taking his arm and pulling
him toward the boat on the water. They waded through the shallows to reach it and the woman, still pulling at the Minstrel's arm,
directed it toward the boat's single sail. It immediately caught fire
and they retreated. Finbar watched in silence.

The boat, wrapped in flames, started sailing by itself toward the
sinking sun. As it burned, silvery smoke rose from the fire and filled

the air with its thick, sweet smell. It stung the Minstrel's eyes and obscured his sight. Nodding on his feet and tired from the day's events and impressions, Finbar dropped to the ground and shut his eyes. Unheeding the sight of the vanishing crowd, he slept alone in the circle of upright stones.

# IV

The first ray of the rising sun fell on Finbar eyelids and woke him up. He rubbed his eyes and sat up, wondering what was happening inside the circle. A distant upright stone on the eastern side of the circle was touched by a golden ray, shone like a jewel, beckoning to Finbar. He started walking toward the easternmost rock, and by the time he reached it, the sun was over the horizon, promising another clear and hot day.

Drawing near the upright stone, he saw at its foot a shallow dig covered with golden straw; on it laid a woman, obviously in labor. She was stark naked, her skin gleaming blinding white. Some women were attending to her, caressing her body and splashing it with water from the stream that ran right through the circle of stones. Other women helped her spiritually, uttering encouraging and comforting words or humming a soothing melody; still others were busy with her surroundings, preparing them for the new mother and son.

As Finbar approached, the laboring woman suddenly stopped in her effort and called out to the Minstrel, "There you are! I've been waiting for you; you know the child cannot be born until you are here to welcome him!" He noticed then that she was the same woman who had helped him kill the victim and burn his body.

"Will she be all right?" he asked someone next to him, who laughed in his face.

"Here he comes, and they are both doing fine, as you can see," she said, pointing out to a picture of mother and son wrapped in golden halo.

"What now, then?" the Minstrel asked.

"Now, we follow the sun," the women sung out and arranged themselves in a process. The sun was climbing up in the sky, and they were parading toward the southernmost side of the circle.

Finbar did not know how long they had been walking. It seemed rather a long time to walk from one side to the other of a circle that could be viewed in one sweeping glance.

But many wonderful things had been happening since he had entered it, and he did not feel like questioning it any more. In the meantime, as they walked on, Finbar noticed that the child had been growing gradually, turning into a boy, then a youth, then a young man that looked very much like the one that had been burned in the boat.

At last, the procession reached the southernmost rock. As they approached the upright stone, the Minstrel noticed that it had assumed the shape of a throne. On that throne sat now the same majestic woman, looking young and glowing with happiness. She was dressed in red, and a golden crown sat on her dark red hair. As the procession drew near, the stone chair widened up and the woman invited the young man to sit on it.

"Here you are, Finbar, just in time to celebrate our wedding. You are the best man to sing us songs and tell us stories, to make this day the happiest in everyone's life."

And so he did. As long as the sun was up in the sky – and to his astonishment, it seemed to stay there a long time indeed – Finbar sang his songs and told his stories, while breaking only for rest and refreshments. At last he grew weary, and a little tipsy from drinking an unusual quantity of wine. His head got dizzy so he shut his eyes; his knees buckled and he fell to the ground, to sleep off the events of the last couple of days.

• • •

When Finbar woke up the next day, the sky was cloudy and threatening with rain. He sat up and found himself by the northern-most stone again, just outside the circle. 'Have I ever been inside it?' he asked himself. "But," he said aloud, "if I haven't, I don't think I'll ever try entering it again."

He rose, put on his coat and threw the bag over his shoulder. Then he started walking, taking care to go round the circle of upright stones rather than walk through it. 'Just the same,' he thought, 'I really have a glorious tale to tell, be it true or a dream I dreamed.'

• • •

# MUSIC, LOVE AND MAGIC

## I

"Why don't you go to the Castle, Finbar?" asked the Farmer's wife. The Minstrel had been staying the night on the farm, filling his belly with the woman's good, sound cooking and granting her and her family a sample of his tales and songs. "They would appreciate your stories even more than we do, perhaps even give you money and presents."

"I don't think that's possible," he grinned at her, being familiar with the tight generosity of the rich. "What can they give me that you haven't, that I really need? Good food, comfortable bed, hearty company, and most of all – an enthusiastic audience." In his memory of castles he had visited in the company of the Old Minstrel, to whom he had been apprentice, with all their glory and finery, the people there were never so friendly as the members of this simple family.

Still, it did not mean he was not going to visit the castle in the vicinity; he always liked to get a variety of audience for his performances, and meet different kinds of people to talk to. So, as he left the farm and its genial people behind him, he walked in the direction that would lead him to the Castle.

• • •

The day was fine; the hilly meadows were green with colorful blossom scattered here and there. As Finbar was feasting his eyes, a strange form gradually appeared in front of them. It was a woman, not very young but quite impressive in appearance, tall and full of body, with curves in the right places. She was covered all over with so many flowers that she seemed actually made of blossoms. Her face looked like it had been carved from the rocks of the hills, and a lively light emanated from her large, brown eyes and her red, glowing lips. Although she looked heavy, she seemed to be floating above the ground, her bare feet barely touching the earth.

"Ah, Finbar," she said, her voice full and throaty, "I see you're going to the Castle."

"Indeed, I am. They say it's the right place for a Minstrel to perform his arts."

"It could be a good place," she nodded, her brown hair moving like waves around her head, "but you should be careful. You never know what might happen in castles..."

"True," Finbar agreed, "but there are people there who may have a use for my arts, as I have a use for them as an audience."

"Indeed," she said, "more than you'd think... Now, why don't you pick the last flower you find on your way there and keep it in your pocket? It could help you in your business at this castle."

"Ha?" The Minstrel looked at her in astonishment; but she was already melting into thin air, vanishing in the same sudden way she had appeared. Finbar shook his head, looked around him, and continued in the direction of the Castle, which loomed dark on a hill at some distance; but as he was looking at it, he felt that the day had darkened, though the sky was still clear of clouds.

When he got nearer, Finbar could see that it was not a very large castle but it looked very old, its stones eroded and darkened by the weather, with a greenish tint from the moss covering them. There were hardly any people outside the walls, and the only animals were one old horse and a couple of sheep. He saw no fields or vegetable patches, and thought that perhaps they were situated on the other side of the Castle. All in all, what he felt about the place was an atmosphere of desolation, as if nobody lived there at all.

Still, the farmers knew that the Castle was inhabited, and he was sure he could rely on them; besides, he just noticed there was a guard behind the locked gate, so he might as well ask him what was going on.

The Minstrel approached the man, who was stocky and heavy-looking and brandished a thick stick in his hand. "Can I come in?" Finbar asked, politely.

"What for? What are you selling?" the guard asked, rudely.

"I am a Minstrel, as you can tell by my appearance; I entertain people with my songs and tales. Don't they like such things in this place?"

The guard looked doubtful, as if he had never encountered a minstrel before. After a moment's hesitation, though, the old ruffian lowered his stick and scratched his head, then said, "When the Old Lady was alive, there was plenty of entertainment here. But now, with the Old Master – " he shook his head and the Minstrel was not sure what he had wanted to express by that movement.

"But if the Old Master is sad about the death of his Lady," he argued, "he may want some entertainment even more, to liven up his days?"

"I'll have to ask the Commander, as it's not a thing I could decide on my own," the guard said at last. "You stay here!" he ordered the Minstrel and turned to go into the yard, leaving the gate locked behind him.

Soon the man came back and said, as he was manipulating the heavy lock, "The Commander of the Guard says you can entertain the servants in the kitchen – they may do with some light in their gloomy life." Then the lock sprang open, the guard pushed the heavy gate, and the Minstrel went in as it was shut behind him.

"I hope you also come to hear me when you're replaced at the gate," he said to the man – it always paid to be polite to people in a position of power. But the guard growled under his thick moustache and only stretched his arm to show the direction for the Minstrel to go into the Castle.

• • •

Closer by, the Castle looked even older and more neglected. There was not one whole stone in its walls, all covered with green slime that seemed to have set there a long time ago. The atmosphere of depression was even heavier now, and the Minstrel walked more and more slowly as he crossed the yard in the direction of the double doors, which stood partly open.

Very few men were in the yard, and Finbar could see that most of them were not ordinary workers but obviously soldiers, busy with their various weapons. Some of them raised their heads to look at the stranger, but none said anything at all, to him or to each other. Keeping silent as well, Finbar quickened his pace, climbed the few steps and entered a dark corridor.

So dark, he could not even see the walls or the distance between them. In front of him, though, Finbar could discern a dim light, toward which he walked now with a quicker pace. He was not actually afraid, but was preparing himself for anything that might happen. Nothing happened, however, and after some minutes of walking, he arrived at the source of light.

The corridor ended with a large hall, opening before the Minstrel a scene of past glory. It was a spacious room hung with beautiful tapestry, with a magnificent candelabra suspended from the high ceiling; here and there stood some elegant furniture, and the floor was made of a beautiful stone mosaic. But the tapestry and the furniture looked decrepit and were covered with dust and cobwebs; the candelabra, empty of candles, had not been polished in ages; and the mosaic floor was crooked and dented in many places, with the scenes it presented on it absurdly distorted. The light, which seemed bright in contrast to the darkness in the corridor, emanated from a few torches hung on the walls that had not been cleaned from smoke and soot for a long time. The desolation seen on the castle's outside was also evident inside.

An old man in servant clothes approached the Minstrel. "The Commander of the Guard has given us notice of your presence here," he croaked. "But the Master cannot see you now. I'll show you the way to the kitchen, where you can eat and rest until you're called by his lordship, if he feels like being entertained."

"It's all the same to me," Finbar made a motion with his arm, "whether my audience is composed of servants or masters, as long as I have one."

The servant did not seem impressed by Finbar's words. With a faint expression of contempt he turned to go, not troubling to see whether the Minstrel was following him or not. He led the way to a staircase at a corner of the Hall, through which they descended on more weathered stones; Finbar had to watch and tread carefully so as not to slip on them. After some twenty stairs, they reached the kitchen, which was better lit than the main hall. The atmosphere here was much more cheerful, crowded with men and women doing their chores, talking and joking among themselves in a lively way.

All the same, it seemed there was not much for them to do, as the Minstrel did not see many provisions they could work with. Two men were halfheartedly plucking feathers off some fowl, but no four-legged animals were being prepared for cooking, either farm or game. A large pot stood over the fire under the supervision of one woman, and he assumed it contained vegetables being cooked. Three women were kneading dough for bread or pastry on the large wooden table standing at the center, and other people were bringing in chopped wood, or carrying water in wooden pails, from the open door at the side of the kitchen.

The servant guiding Finbar turned to one of the kneading women and said, "Sara, you take care of this man." Then he turned to go back up the stairs.

• • •

Sara was a tall, thin woman, her movements energetic and her eyes lively. "Sit," she ordered the Minstrel; "here is bread and cheese and a cup of ale. While you eat, you can tell us who you are and how come they have let you into the Castle. We don't see many strangers here these days."

Finbar sat down, broke the bread and cheese and sipped from the ale, wiped his lips and sighed in pleasure. "I am a minstrel," he said, "I've come to amuse you with songs and tales."

"Ha ha," another woman burst out laughing, "he's come to the Castle to tell tales! We can tell you some tales of our own, if you want!"

"Shush, Nillie," Sara ordered. "He does not know us and there's no need to tell him wild tales."

"No," Finbar agreed, "I've come from a long way away and indeed, I have been told it's not easy to amuse the people here, in this Castle. Has it got a name, by the way?"

Two men, who had put chopped wood in the corner, came and sat at the table, filling their cups with ale. They and the women looked now at the Minstrel with what seemed to him a meaningful gaze.

"They used to call it 'The Joy of the Hills'," said one of the men, "but that was before the Old Lady died."

"Now we call it 'The Gloom of the Hills', since…" a woman began and stopped, turning her attention back to the dough.

"Don't work so hard, Sheril," Sara told her softly, "you'll get the bread too sour. Let's put it aside now, to rise."

The three women folded the kneaded dough to one lump, put it on the side of the table and covered it with cloth. Then they gathered at the table and sat down. "Only for one cup of ale," Sara warned them, "we still have much to do."

"I can't see why we have to work so hard, when there's not even one piece of game to prepare for dinner," one of the men complained.

"There's always something to do, and you should go back to work, Gavin. Get up, then, get away with you." She shooed the men out with a movement of her arm, then sat down by the Minstrel's side, poured herself a cup of ale and broke a piece of bread. "So, give us some of the treasure in your bag to amuse us, Minstrel," she said, pleasantly, "for I'm not sure you'll be able to reach the Master for that purpose."

"Something happened, then, since the Old Lady died, as I hear?" he asked.

"Not just the Old Lady," another woman remarked – Finbar thought she was the one called Sheril – "the young one as well..." Sheril was prettier than Sara, younger and with bright, light-color hair peeping from under her work bonnet, and shining blue eyes. "After the Old Lady died of an illness, no one was looking after her daughter Helena, who was a beautiful girl and was going to marry the son of the Commander of the Guard. One day they went hunting together, the Young Lady's horse started galloping wildly, she fell off, hit her head and died. In my opinion, that's when all the troubles began."

"What are you talking about?" another woman cried out. "Helena has not died, she's been lying in bed for months, still breathing. That's why she can't be buried, though she looks dead. Her nurse Cora is taking care of her."

"But how can she live, without eating and drinking?" Sheril demanded.

"The nurse manages from time to time to get her to drink beer or milk. Indeed, I've heard that she's got very thin, and is not as beautiful as she used to be," the woman answered.

"I see you know it all, Bertha, so tell us, what's happening with Gerard, the son of the Commander of the Guard?" asked Sara with interest. "I heard he is not the man he used to be, always cheerful and good hearted."

Bertha's face clouded. She was older than the other two, her hair gray and her face wrinkled, and the Minstrel wondered why the younger Sara was in charge of the kitchen work and not she. But Sara's eyes expressed a great deal of energy, while Bertha's were dim and weary looking. "I know what Cora tells me when she comes to fetch something for the Master's daughter. But when I asked her about Gerard, she would not answer. I have a feeling something very bad has happened to that young man."

"What d'you think, Sara?" Sheril turned to her boss. "I have an idea you've always liked him, haven't you? Maybe now you can realize your dream with him?"

"Shut up, Sheril, you don't know what you're talking about. Bertha is right, I know something terrible has happened to him but I don't know what…" She fell silent, and for a few moments the whole kitchen was quiet. Then she recovered and started giving new orders to the workers, who rose and turned to their various chores. Sara turned to Finbar, "What do they call you, Minstrel? We'll have to find you a place to rest and sleep at night, for you can't use any of the guest rooms of the Castle."

"They call me Finbar. But d'you think there's any chance for doing my performance upstairs tonight, after all that I've heard here?"

"I can't say. But if you can't go to them, we'll be very happy to listen to you here – unless it's beneath your dignity?"

Finbar laughed. "There's no difference to me who listens to my words and music - masters or servants – as long as they're ready to hear me at all."

"Good," Sara said, giving him a sympathetic gaze. She then led him to a niche in one of the kitchen's walls, which contained a stone bench, and signed for him to put his bag there. "I'll bring you a blanket if you haven't got one, and as long as the weather holds you can wash in the stream down below," she pointed toward the open kitchen's door. "If it changes, we have enough water in the kitchen, and perhaps you can help us bring in some more."

"Gladly," the Minstrel replied, "I don't object to doing anything useful, as long as you haven't got time to listen to my tales and songs."

## II

At sunset, the servants gathered in the kitchen for dinner from all parts of the Castle. About twenty people sat at the large wooden table taking part in a meal of stewed vegetables with offal, bread, ale and a few fruits; there was enough for all and filling enough, if not particularly rich. The Minstrel talked little and mainly listened to what was said, in particular what was told about the goings on at the Castle. He was bothered by the sketchy words he caught and did not know what to think about them.

Toward the end of the meal, when the Castle's servants were still sitting with their cups of ale and the kitchen workers had risen to clear the table and wash the dishes, the weather clouded over, the wind stirred and soon after it started raining. At that time, the nurse Cora came down the stairs, approached the Minstrel and told him he was called to amuse the masters at the Castle's hall.

Without delay, Finbar followed her up the stairs and entered the big hall. It was better lit at this hour; candles were alight in candlesticks on the tables scattered around, and a greater number of torches hung on the walls. But the great candelabra remained dark.

Finbar, happy for the lights, was astonished to see the hall almost empty of people. A young man came to meet him, tall and handsome with dark hair, finely cut face and dark blue eyes. But the beautiful eyes seemed empty, no living light shone in them, as if his very soul had been extinguished. His voice sounded dead as well, when he invited Finbar to approach the corner where a few people were bunched together.

"I am Gerard," the young man said, then presented the other people sitting in the hall's corner. "This is my father Rolf, Commander of the Guard; and this is my mother, Xenia, the Castle's housekeeper," he said in a monotonous voice.

The two of them bowed their heads before the Minstrel but did not rise, and Finbar noticed the woman's worried face. Her husband's face was blank of emotions, but he sensed anger clouding the man's light-colored eyes. The young man moved toward another man, who was sitting in a deep armchair; perhaps in the distant past he had looked a handsome figure of a man, but now he was shrunk and lifeless. The man did not look at the approaching Minstrel, nor was he looking anywhere else, but seemed only to gaze inside himself, as if pondering on his fate, unable to waken from his reflections.

"This is Lord Manning, the Castle's Master," Gerard said in his dead voice, "and this," he continued to the other side of the Master, "this is – " at this point he faltered, as if he had lost his words and was unable to present the man before him. Finbar looked with interest at that man, who was sitting in a straight-back chair, whose personality had such a deadly effect on young Gerard. The man rose from his seat, looming to an unusual height, and his body looked unnaturally thin under the dark, wide cloak he was wearing. His hair was long, falling to his shoulders and mixing with the long beard that grew down to his chest. His thick brows covered his eyes, which seemed like two black holes in his gaunt face.

"This," the man said in a voice that echoed throughout the Castle, "is Cosmo the Great, and don't let anyone mislead you to think otherwise."

For a moment Finbar felt as if he was being hypnotized by the gaze of the black eyes; then he shook his head, dispersing the fog that was beginning to gather in his mind. In a clear and pleasant voice he said, "Aye, Cosmo," his voice almost singing the words. "I have a feeling I've heard about you and your enormous power."

"Then," said the man as he sat down again, "perhaps you can amuse us with the tales you've heard about Cosmo and his great power."

"I would be happy to do it, providing I could accompany my song with some instrument; I have lost a couple of strings on mine, and will have to reach a less lonesome place to replace them. Is there any kind of string instrument in this Castle?" He turned his question to the world at large.

To his astonishment, the answer came as Cosmo turned to the son of the Commander of the Guard, "Gerard, fetch the Minstrel your guitar," he ordered, adding with a sneer, "you are not using it these days, anyway, are you?"

"Your son can sing?" Finbar asked the Commander and his wife.

The woman's face darkened even more, while her husband answered, "He used to, once, but not since Helena was hurt; she's lying in her bed, barely alive, and can't listen to him any more. They are betrothed, you know?"

"Were betrothed!" corrected Cosmo with a sneer.

"So I've heard," Finbar replied, looking sympathetically at the young man. "Is there no cure to her illness?"

"Cora is doing her best," the housekeeper replied with doubt. "It would be better if we could send to the nearest city for a doctor and some good medicine, but –"

The Commander lay his hand on his wife's knee and she fell silent. Absentmindedly, Finbar put his hand into his pocket and felt in it something unusually soft to the touch; he took his hand out and found himself holding the rosy blossom he had picked on the way at the suggestion of the Flower woman. Something stirred in his heart as he looked at it, a tune sang itself in his mind and he knew what he was going to play for his audience.

As the Minstrel put the flower back in his pocket, Gerard returned with a guitar in his hand. Finbar took it and admired its beauty; it was made of the best wood and seemed to be well taken care of. Stroking the strings, Finbar strummed a chord; finding them too loose, as if not being played for a long time, he tightened them and listened for a moment to their fine tune. Then he strummed a proper chord, played an introductory tune and began his tale.

Once there was a wizard, who was neither old nor young but ageless. He was a great scholar with much experience in magic, who could do anything he liked everywhere he went. But he was a very ugly and wicked man, and he could never make any young and pretty girl fall in love with him; and for some mysterious reason, that had become his sole ambition in life. So he set on his travels, searching for the one young and pretty girl who would succumb to his magic and fall in love with him.

Everywhere the wizard went left traces of his magical, evil deeds; but nowhere did he find the sort of magic that would make a young and pretty girl fall in love with him. Then, one day he reached a castle, where a noble widower lived with his young and pretty daughter, who was betrothed to the son of the Commander of the Guard. The nobleman, constantly in mourning over his good and wise wife, received the wizard into his castle without recognizing his evil power. The wizard decided to use this power and marry the girl even if she did not fall in love with him. That would compensate his wicked heart for the lack of the love he craved for.

First, he directed his magic against the young man, casting over him such a spell that his heart was sealed against the whole world, and particularly against his own love. That indifferent attitude from her lover caused the girl to fall from her horse, become ill and shun the world as she sank into a deep coma; next, the wizard made her father, the castle's master, powerless in his own domain, sinking deeply under the wizard's spell and getting ready to give him his daughter for wife.

Who, then, is going to set out against the evil wizard and rescue the innocent people from his clutches?

With a flourish of a great accord on the strings, the Minstrel stopped his song-tale at this questioning tone.

Silence fell throughout the big hall. For one moment it seemed to Finbar that the lights were dimming, as if all the candles were extinguished. Then Cosmo rose, and Finbar thought, 'He is the wizard in the story, full of power, and how can I stand against him?' But he kept standing where he was without moving, his face turning toward the wizard, who now raised his hand. In it, he was holding a short wand, and as he moved it, the storm broke into the Hall from outside. The wind blasted around the Hall, creating havoc; lightning raged, flying everywhere, causing burns on furniture and raising the hair on people's heads. Heavy fog lay on furniture and people, who started coughing, choking on their breath. Freezing cold took hold of everyone, making them shiver in physical and mental misery.

Fighting against his own suffering, Finbar raised his hand and hit the strings of the guitar. The storm halted for a moment, the lightning dimmed. Then the wizard raised his wand again, and the turmoil resumed with more strength. Again the Minstrel made the chord, calming the storm, and again the wizard answered with his own power. Thus the war raged between music and magic, with both sides ignoring their surroundings, concentrating on using their powers, which seemed equal with no one the stronger or the weaker.

But there was a difference between the two powers. Finbar knew he was fighting for people's lives, while the wizard only fought to achieve his desires. In the end, he had to reach the conclusion that the effort was not worth the result. At last, his hand dropped and his hold on his wand relaxed. Making a last gesture, he turned the wand on himself, enchanting his own body into a turning top, twirling round and round, faster and faster, until he turned himself into a storm that rose and flew toward an open window and outside into the wide world.

For a moment, there was nothing but silence and stillness. The storm was gone, the sky cleared; the light returned to the candles and the torches and the flying dust settled down. Only the upheaval in the hall remained, and a bunch of people sitting, stunned, in a corner.

• • •

It was the old Master who suddenly woke from his reverie. "What was it? What's happened? What are you doing here, Gerard, without Helena? And who is that man there, holding your guitar?"

The Commander of the Guard rose from his seat, approached Lord Manning and kneeled before him. "Sir, don't you remember what happened to you since this terrible man came here?"

"What terrible man? What are you talking about? Is it the one holding the guitar? He does not seem so bad to me…"

"No, he is the one who saved us from the wizard who had put a spell on you, on my son and on your daughter. Xenia," he turned to his wife, "I think you may go now and see about Helena, I have a feeling…"

The housekeeper rose and left the hall. "Gerard?" the Commander turned to his son.

"I am all right now, father," the young man said in a soft voice, and Finbar saw his blue eyes shining as he had not seen them before. "I knew what was happening to me but I could not stop it! It was terrible, father, you can't imagine…" And the Minstrel heard a choking weeping in his voice. "If anything happened to Helena, I could never forgive myself."

"You know it was not your fault, Gerard, but I'm glad you feel like yourself again," said his father and hugged his son.

"But what was all that about. Explain it to me, Rolf!" the Master of the Castle ordered.

"It was a wizard who came here, wanting to take over, Sir. He sealed your own soul and my son's to anything in the world, and made your Lady Daughter fall off her horse and lose her consciousness. I hope she will recover now."

"But how did you overcome him?" the Old Master asked.

"Not us – we were powerless against the wizard. It was this Minstrel, here," he pointed at Finbar, who was still standing with the guitar in his hand.

"A Minstrel, eh?" the Master turned to him with interest. "I love music, and Gerard here used to make our nights pleasant with his songs. But I never knew you could fight magic with music."

"Neither did I," said Finbar and bowed his head before the Master. "But I think there was probably another force in action here."

"What d'you mean?" asked the Master. At that moment he turned his head and cried out, "Helena! You're all right! Come to me, Daughter, I have a feeling I haven't seen you for a long time."

Finbar looked at the young woman who appeared at the door in the company of the housekeeper; she looked far from her former glorious appearance, but in her face the Minstrel was able to discern the other force that helped him win the fight against the wicked wizard – the force of love.

• • •

# THE MAGIC WAR

## I

"I will not believe in Magic!" said Cornell emphatically. He was a tallish man of twenty-eight, with indistinguishable features in soft brown colors. His main strength lay in two areas: his chosen profession of a statistician, and his love for his family.

His twin sister Neila laughed. "You won't believe there is magic in your numbers, then?" she teased. She was much more assertive in her features than her brother; tall for a woman with a shock of wavy auburn hair and lively green eyes. Having dropped from college and tried various jobs, she was now a student witch and proud of her dealing with magic.

Neila and Cornell Rodin, with his wife and child, had come to their parents' apartment in town for the occasion of their mother's birthday. In a way, the parents' characters were more pronounced than their children's. Louise Rodin had delayed middle age with her free spirit and liveliness, which exceeded that of Neila's; in looks, the mother seemed to have served as the mould for her daughter.

Louise knew her mind better than Neila, and had continually occupied herself with the curio shop named Hecate's Place, which she had kept for many years. She had inherited some money that helped her in this venture, which her husband's salary could not have done, especially in acquiring new merchandise that came her way. Paul Rodin was a history professor at the local college and during the years had specialized in the history of magic. He was taller and heavier than his son, his brown coloring more definite, and his whole appearance impressed even his opponents in Academy.

"Actually," Clare, Cornell's little wife, said in her soft, sweet voice, "I see magic in everything in the world. Mountains, and springs, the sea and the moon; but mainly in life..." She looked like a magical being herself, with her golden hair and soft blue eyes, lovely face and beautiful figure. She was holding tight to her body their two year old daughter, whom she had named Charm, in spite of her husband's silent but clear displeasure. So strong was his mental objection, that he had never called the child by name, addressing her only by titles of endearment.

"Let's not get into that old argument," Louise interrupted in her decisive voice. "It's my birthday and I want peace and quiet. So, who wants more cake?"

• • •

The Great Wizard Kindrik – a title he had given himself, though other people actually thought him quite powerful – was contemplating his next move. He was a big man with thick black hair streaming from his head in constant disorder, many times used for a great magical effect. His face was dark and craggy with a large nose, thin lips and a big mouth, and deep-sitting black eyes.

'How can I fulfill my goal in life in destroying all witches in the world?' he asked himself. He gazed into the mirrors that paneled his studio of magic, trying to find out the best object for that purpose.

The Great Wizard Kindrik had by now existed for endless centuries, and he was beginning to be bored with many of the magical works that had occupied him through the ages. Looking back at the deeds he had accomplished in his life, and in spite of congratulating himself on his many feats of magic, he was searching for a change.

Nevertheless, in spite of himself he was looking at one such feat that was frustrated by a strange rival. He had not even heard of that minstrel three or four hundred years ago, Finbar by name, until he happened to visit that particular castle where Kindrik had been working his magic to further his own ends. The Wizard had enchanted the daughter of the house, having put a hindrance charm over her parents and her betrothed, hoping to marry her and acquire all the family possessions with not too much effort. And here came a plain, miserable minstrel, a stooping elderly man in tatters and not even a magician in any way, who, with his music – HIS MUSIC! – blocked all the wizard's efforts.

Kindrik gave in then and disappeared from that site, only to surface from time to time to do his worst evil deeds possible. In the last hundred years he had found some entertainment in working against modern witches who were trying to use their magic in the benefit of humanity. The Wizard had been playing havoc with the weather, killing the patients of healers and poisoning waters and plants, until many of those witches despaired and were forced to forsake their good deeds.

But he was getting tired of that also. Not wanting to start feeling old, as he was fearing in his heart of heart, he was searching for some special feat that would allow him to abandon the world of the living with an unforgettable flourish. He had decided to put a final end to witches and their progeny all over the world. His idea was for the first time more on the line of quantity rather than quality. 'Yes,' he thought to himself, 'he was going to take on whole groups known for their witching powers, render them completely impotent or eliminate them altogether.'

Kindrik looked through his Mirror of Knowledge. Deliberating who he was going to attack first, his mental gaze fell on the Rodin family. Many members of that family had powers, though some of them unacknowledged. They were also such people that were thought to be helpful for the ones in need, an idea that was an anathema to Kindrik the Wizard. 'Acting against such a potentially powerful group,' he reflected, 'would give me an enormous satisfaction I have not felt for a long time.'

• • •

"I feel something's wrong but I can't tell what," Neila confided in Elinor. There was a friendly rivalry between Louise and Elinor, who kept a shop of more definitely mystic artifacts than the haphazard mixture that filled Louise's store. Unlike the distinguished looking Louise, with her tall stature, gleaming blond hair arranged artfully and piercing blue eyes, Elinor was a heavy, plump woman of middle height, with soft brown eyes; her hair, though, was colored with stripes and elaborately done, but not as artistic as Louise's. They were of the same middle age, but Louise looked at least ten years younger.

Still, it was to Elinor that Neila turned when she felt herself troubled by anything. This time, though, she was not able to define that trouble. "I feel restless," the girl said, "I don't know why. As if I expect something, may be something horrible, to happen any minute. It's funny, isn't it? What horrible thing can happen to us this day and age?"

"Well –" said Elinor.

Neila did not let her friend continue. "I never think of terrible things, you know. I enjoy living my life, I have friends, I study what's interesting to me; I've even started learning how to use my powers; so, why should I think anything terrible is going to happen? But still." She paused this time, breathing deeply.

"Are you doing anything besides studying magic?" Elinor asked in the lull that occurred.

"Oh, I'm doing waitressing at that little café, you know. They don't pay much, just enough to live in the little flat I share with other witch students. We eat very cheaply, and I hardly ever have to come home except to wash my clothes and such. It's such a good, free life and I've nothing to complain about, so why do I have that feeling of coming horror? I almost can't stand it now!"

Tears came into her eyes, shining blue like her mother's, and for a moment Elinor was lost for words. "You know," Neila added; "I went to see Mother at her store, right in the middle of work. I don't care if they fire me. I was just looking around, idle like, you know, and I saw that funny little statue or more like statuette because it was rather small. I think you'd like to see it because I definitely felt the magic in it."

"Really? A magical statuette? I would like to see it. What was it like?"

"A man with a crane. Chinese, it looked to me; you know how they are with those details." Owing to her many visits to her mother's and Elinor's stores, Neila was quite familiar with objects of art and folk craft.

"I see that I'll have to see it with my own eyes," Elinor said.

"Come, let's take a look. Aren't you closing for lunch?"

"Not really, but I can leave Shina here for a moment. I'll tell her not to sell anything, just wait for me to come back." She called the girl, who had been cleaning the shelves, gave her instructions and the two of them left to go to Louise Rodin's curiosity shop. Elinor was quite aware that Neila had failed to elaborate on her trouble, but thought that new object might merit such a distraction.

• • •

"How lovely!" Neila exclaimed as the three of them crowded in front of the shelf where the statuette was standing. "It is Chinese, isn't it?"

Louise took the artifact and put it on a table, so that all three women could look at it better. It was small, about 12cm high; it showed a man in an upright position, holding a flute to his lips and raising one foot as if dancing. Behind the man and somewhat upward, stood a crane on one foot, its head pulled back with its beak raised upward; its wings were spread over the man's head, ready to take off in a flight. The man's head was also pulled back with his eye on the bird, as if taking his cue from it.

"It's as if the bird – a crane, isn't it? – serves as the man's inspiration," remarked Louise. "I have heard that cranes have that quality."

"I can almost hear the tune the man hears, making me want to dance as well," Neila whispered.

"I can see why you think it may have magic powers," said Elinor. "Where did you get it, Louise?"

"It was brought in by some new immigrants, trying to make a little money to help them settle here," Louise explained, "I think they had some vague idea of its being rather more than a common piece of folklore, because I couldn't afford to pay the price they wanted; you know I only deal with inexpensive trinkets. But I still can't make up my mind about it. Do you think it's real magic, then, Neila? And what'd you say, Elinor? Could it be worth a great deal of money?"

"I say that we need the opinion of a better expert than me to decide," Elinor said, turning the figurine over and over, as if looking for a clue to its essence.

"Whose opinion would you take, then?" asked Louise.

"I have a friend who has great knowledge," said Elinor. "She should at least know more than I do, or who we can really ask."

"Knowledge of art or of magic?" asked Louise; "because if it's art, I know a few knowledgeable people myself."

"Magic, of course; she's a witch," replied Elinor. "At least, she would know whether this is magical or not."

"A witch? Would Neila know her?" Unlike her daughter, and in spite of habitually using her natural intuitive powers, Louise had never gone into the actual world of magic.

"Mother!" Neila intervened. "Who is it, Elinor? I know I'm just a beginner, but I do know a few witches."

"Ofara, have you heard of her?" Elinor asked.

"I have, though I've never met her," answered Neila. "She's well known among our people." She was proud to use that epithet as if she had belonged for ever to that magical world.

"So you think that friend of yours can give me really good advice about this figurine?" Louise asked, happy to get the responsibility of what seemed to be a highly priced object off her hands.

"I'll bring her along," Elinor promised. "Besides being knowledgeable, she's also a very clever woman and always ready with good advice."

"All right," Louise agreed, and Elinor left, hurrying back to her own shop. The mother then turned to her daughter. "Now, what is it, Neila? I suppose you have quit your job again, coming here in the middle of the day?"

"Never mind that job, I must talk to you. I have a feeling it's important, and it can even be connected somehow or other with this figurine."

"Really? Let's get some lunch, then, and hear about it in comfort. I suppose you'll stay until that Ofara comes, won't you?"

"Leave off, Mother," Neila said. "I hope you'll at least be polite to her."

"I'm always polite, to whomever it is I talk to," her mother protested. "But I do hope you'll stick to something sometimes, you've been changing interests the way I change my clothes."

"No." Neila's voice sounded unusually definite and decisive, and Louise looked at her daughter as if seeing her for the first time. She had changed, seemed more settled in this new interest. Well, the mother thought, as long as it lasts and doing no visible harm, she would let it be and keep her good relations with her daughter.

The two of them entered the back room, which was quite spacious and furnished with comfortable sitting. There were facilities for washing with running cold and hot water, a fridge for light meals, a couple of chairs and a small table. They were finishing their cheese, salad and coffee when the doorbell rang and Neila went to see who was coming.

She knew she had seen Ofara before as soon as she lay her eyes on the short, rounded, dark woman that passed through entered the store. She felt subject to an examining dark gaze that seemed to be piercing her innermost being. "You are Neila, the novice, aren't you?" she said in a surprisingly warm voice that dissipated her rather intimidating appearance.

Neila nodded, and proceeded to present Louise, who had come out of the back room. "I like your place," she said, her eyes roving, "though I don't think I've ever been inside it. So, what is it about that statue Elinor was talking about? I'm not at all an expert on art or artifacts, you know."

"Here it is," Louise showed her the figurine. "Elinor said you might know someone who is an expert."

"So I do," the Witch replied, as she took hold of the artifact and looked at it closely. "I can feel the magic in my fingertips," she whispered. "Was that what Elinor meant, Neila?"

The girl nodded, still a little overwhelmed.

"Who is that expert?" asked Louise.

"You must know him yourself, as you have a personal connection with College through your husband. It's the curator of the College Museum."

"D'you mean that funny Dr. Green?" asked Louise. "I have seen him sometime or other, but I've never had a chance to talk to him. Isn't he a little strange? I never felt like taking him seriously as an expert."

"He may be a little strange in his mannerisms," agreed Ofara, "but we've been friends for years, and he's enormously knowledgeable and worth talking to. I'm not sure he would know about this object being magical or not, because he hasn't any powers himself, but he'd certainly understand its essential value."

"Do you think he'd have the funds to buy it, if that is so?" Louise asked.

"I know he has some sources but I don't know what they are," the Witch smiled. "I'm almost sure he will want to buy it himself, and in that case, he'll know where to get the funds for it."

• • •

At noon the next day Louise closed Hecate's Place and she, Ofara and Neila went by appointment to the Museum, taking the little statue with them. The curator, Dr. Green, was a portly man in his fifties, with fading fair hair and piercing gray eyes; he greeted his old friend Ofara with affectionate words, but immediately turned his eager expression toward the new exciting object in front of him.

"This is wonderful!" he announced; "this is priceless! And don't worry about the money, Mrs. Rodin, it will be regarded as an investment," he added.

"Do you, then, understand the meaning of this group?" she asked.

"It is a combination," he explained slowly, "of poetic inspiration expressed by the crane bird, and dance music as shown by the man and his flute. This is as clear an expression of magic as I've ever seen in a physical presentation. I'm going to show it to other, knowledgeable people, but there's no doubt it should have its honorable place at the Museum."

"Indeed, I had a feeling –" Louise started when Neila interrupted her mother, "That's exactly it!" she cried out. "And it's the kind of magic that could be of great help in trouble."

"Trouble?" Louise said to her, sharply. "What'd you mean by that?"

"I – I am not sure, quite," Neila stammered, not knowing what to say. After all, this was just a vague feeling she had had, and she was unable to express it in words. And now, she had got the same sense from her mother, who had never even acknowledged herself as a witch.

"My friend Ofara –" Dr. Green said, "She said something or other of this kind, but I didn't listen to her very closely. Many of the artifacts here are connected with magic, but I don't always know for sure what they are about. So, this is a helpful little article, isn't it? Well, you can always come here for help if you need it, you know."

"Thank you," Louise said, "Come on, Neila, I must get back to the shop. This thing is safe here, isn't it, Dr. Green?" she asked the man with some anxiety, "and I'll get the money to pay the owners, as you said?"

"Don't worry about any of this," he said; "We have a very good security system here, so it should be safe," he promised, as he accompanied them outside, having deposited the statuette inside the safe in his office.

## II

The Great Wizard Kindrik sat in his lonesome place of habitation, reflecting his dark thoughts. It was actually a castle, a numerous centuries old, remnant of what used to be a nobleman's fortress against the horde of medieval lawless men. It was built from the local stones of the mountain, where it was situated near its top, and actually formed an integral part of that rocky ground, with which it was now merged almost completely.

The Wizard was virtually as old as the building. In his many adventures, always occupied with the latest magical means to enhance his power, he had found the way of extending his life indefinitely.

"Control," he was saying in his harsh, hoarse voice to the poisonous black toad with yellow warts that was his companion for many years, "is the best stock in trade I could have chosen. Control of Nature, of people, even of historical events – there is no limit. And now I've began on that greatest of all missions, the control of all magic on earth. It will be my last and biggest feat yet, and I shall be forever remembered as the most powerful wizard that had ever lived!"

He allowed the toad to crack, the hoarse sound answering to that of the wizard's. Lately, he had been feeling the need to rest after such long speech, and catch his sometimes failing breath, before he could continue.

"If you want to be great, my friend," he croaked, hate dripping from his lips like fluid poison, "you have to be as unscrupulous as you need to. Witchcraft has become the fashion in this impossible modern world, no longer persecuted. Ah, the lost days of the Inquisition! They were able to use me in those days, to direct them to those hidden practitioners of that abominable Art."

Kindrik had always hated witches, especially the female ones. They used such an unfair competition! Do-gooders, always trying to help people; and healers! That's not the proper way to use power, he thought. Now it seemed that even the Great Inquisition had never been able to eradicate witches from humanity. "It's my task, then, to do it," he told himself, "even on my own. I'm still strong enough for that. I shall do it, if it is my last mission on earth!"

At last, those thoughts were too much even for a strong and powerful being like Kindrik the Wizard; at the end of this speech he had to take a long rest, while planning to the last detail the great job of destruction that was before him.

• • •

When they were leaving the Museum, Louise invited Ofara to come and spend the evening with the Rodins at their apartment. "I'm glad you could come," Louise said to the Witch, as Neila was serving refreshments; "it was so good of you to help me with that Chinese artifact, I really didn't know what to do with it, as I couldn't ask the amount it was worth from my regular customers. I can now help that immigrant family more than I would have been able to

– they are such nice people, and I didn't think they realized what treasure they had in their hands."

Both Paul and Neila were home when Ofara came in the evening, and Louise presented her husband and the Witch to each other. Ofara had actually met Professor Rodin, having taken his class of History of Magic; but he could barely remember her, as Ofara had always been a self-effacing person and did not like to attract attention.

"Has my course been helpful to you, then?" Paul asked, as he realized the Witch had been his student.

"Yes," she said, "quite helpful. It's always good to know more about your business than you actually need to use. Especially the background."

"Business?" he wondered.

"You have to be in some sort of business if you want to make a living, Father, even if you are a witch. Don't you, Ofara?" Neila said.

"But what does it mean to be a witch, in these days of widespread technology?" he insisted.

"Most commercial doings are really trivial for a practicing witch," Ofara answered with a wink in her eye. "You know, astrology, and such, or prescriptions for natural remedies, which I don't really do. But sometimes you are called for in real trouble, and this usually does not pay much, on the whole, unless your clients are well off and they like to compensate a person for taking the trouble to help."

The Professor fell silent for a while, and Louise took over, talking about her shop and of various interesting artifacts in it. "In confirmation of what Ofara has said, it's really the simpler artifacts which bring the most money; the more significant ones are very difficult to sell because most people don't understand such significance."

"What, for instance?" asked her daughter with interest. Since taking the subject of witchcraft seriously, she found out she had a lot to learn; clearly, knowing about powerful magical object was one of these things.

"I once had a necklace," her mother said, "not as pretty as most people would like to have, but I was told by some people it was quite powerful."

"In what way?"

"The beads were carved from olive wood, very fancy but not to everyone's taste. Its magic was connected with fertility, as the olive tree is one of the most ancient talismans in the world."

"That sounds like a farfetched idea," remarked her husband.

"Even if you remember Athena's gift to Athens?" Ofara commented.

"Well, I would never apply it to modern life," said the Professor of History.

"People haven't changed that much since those days," Louise shrugged. "Some people take magic very seriously, while others see only the outside prettiness. That is why I don't mind selling both kinds, unlike those mystic shops, like Elinor's, which insisted on real magic as far as they are aware of it."

When the Witch rose to go, Neila offered to take her home in her car. While going, the girl said, "Have you felt something in the air, Ofara? Something which has not been right, lately?"

Ofara was silent for a moment. "You're right, there's something that I can't put a finger on. Still, as long as we don't know what it is, we can do nothing but wait and see."

"Do you think it may be connected with that statue?"

"Not exactly, but it does come into it somehow. I'd like to see it placed at the Museum. Say, why don't you get your family to go there in the weekend; I'm sure the rest of them would be interested to see it in its proper place."

"You think they may all be affected by what's coming?" Neila asked, worrying.

"Isn't that what you're afraid of?" replied Ofara with a question.

• • •

Ofara came early to the Museum on Sunday, going directly to Dr. Green's office. "Well, Sam," she said, taking a chair on the other side of his desk.

"Ofara," he acknowledged her. "What can I do for you?"

"I'd like to hear what you've learned about that Chinese figurine we brought to you the other day."

"You do, don't you? Is it of any importance to you?"

"It might be, and particularly to the women of the Rodin family who brought it to you."

"Indeed? You know I met the people who owned it. They were sent to me by Mrs. Rodin."

"Did you pay them for it? They only wanted to sell it for the money they needed to settle down here."

"I paid them well, as it happened, because I'd just got a good donation. They have no more claims on it, for which I am quite happy."

"Did they tell you anything about it, then?"

"Some history but not much. It belonged to the woman's grandmother, who had inherited it from her grandmother. A long history, you may say, but I'm not sure of its significance."

"Didn't she tell you of any stories about it?"

"Of course she did. You know how these things are. Many tall tales about magic and miracles, of which she barely believed, having grown up in the Communist regime and not exactly a believer in any kind of magic, or even religion of any sort."

"I see. That's good, in a way, I didn't want the truth to come out about it."

"The truth? Do you know anything?"

"I felt it when I held it. There's much more than tall tales connected with that figurine, but I don't want to be specific. Let's get into the Hall of Artifacts; I'd like to take another look at it; and I've fixed to meet again the Rodin family there around noon today."

"You always bring strange people here for me to meet, don't you, Ofara?" Dr. Green grumbled, but he came out with the Witch, nonetheless.

"Nonsense," said the Witch. "Anyway, you must know Prof. Rodin from College."

"Ah, here you are, Ofara," said Neila as the two came into the Hall. Prof. Rodin nodded to her and to the Curator; he then presented his son Cornell, who had his daughter Charm with him, and Ofara was impressed with the young man's reserved attitude, keeping any hint of possible magical quality in his character in strict check, away from any curious and sensitive person.

"Where are the rest of you?" asked the Witch.

"Mother and Clare went to the Hecate's Place for a moment," Neila explained; "Mother wanted Clare to see something she had recently bought. They'll be here in a few moments. Have you been here before, Cornell?" she asked her brother.

"Not recently," he answered curtly, "we came here when I was at school." He looked around him with a closed expression, belying the wonders that filled the place.

The museum's Hall of Artifacts was full of strange and fantastic exhibits, mostly quite old or even ancient, some of them well known for being connected with magic. There was, for instance, a silver wand which had belonged to a Hindu wizard, with a grand emerald at its top carved with just one letter in Sanskrit. There was a golden hand – Hamsa – from Morocco, with Hebrew letters on it against the evil eye. There was the shrunken head of a monkey from the Amazon area, with pictorial markings carved on it rather than letters. Then there was an ancient Mesopotamian parchment with astrological signs in pictures and cuneiforms lettering. A central piece was an enormous garnet jewel, on which some mysterious script was carved; but the Chinese figurine, though not at the center of the Hall, was allowed a place of honor by itself, in a case of armored glass.

Ofara saw Cornell, whom she had not yet met, lifting his daughter Charm to take a closer look at the statuette. The child stretched both hands toward the artifact, and both the Curator and the Witch stopped dead at the sight, staring. A shaft of light came out of the artifact directed onto Charm's hands and, without any change in the state of the case, she was holding the figurine in her hands.

Charm laughed gaily and her father, stunned, took her away and sat down on a chair, put her on his knees and said in a strangled voice, "How did you do it?" he asked severely. "What did you do? Now we'll have to put it back and I don't know how!"

Dr. Green came up to them and said in his kindest voice, "Now, I've seen a few miracles in my time but never anything like that. Did you see it, Ofara? What do you think?"

"I think there's a ray of hope when things get too dark for us."

"What do you mean by that? What things get too dark and what'd you need a ray of hope for?" the Curator asked, astonished at her words.

"I'm not sure yet, but something very bad is coming, and I can see that both this child and that statue are going to be of great help."

"You think I should give the figurine to that family? After I paid all that money for it?" said the upset Dr. Green.

"Not at all, it would do no good now, before anything happens," she assured him. Indeed, they had no difficulty in retrieving the statuette from the child, as she accompanied her father; they continued to move about the Hall, looking at the other artifacts and talking quietly together.

• • •

Dr. Green put the statuette back in its case, and he and Ofara joined Paul Rodin and his daughter. Neila said, then, "I was wondering about that garnet jewel, Dr. Green. Father does not know anything about it so I wanted to ask you."

The Curator smiled secretively at Ofara and said, "It was lost once, and Ofara helped to recover it, but I don't think we have time now for that story. Did you see what that child had done with the Chinese figurine? Did you know she had such powers?"

"Her mother did not call her Charm for nothing," said the young aunt. At that moment, Louise appeared at the Hall of Artifacts in a state of great agitation. "Paul," she cried out, "has Clare come in yet? Where is Cornell and Charm? I'm afraid something terrible may have happen and I'm not sure what it is or what we can do about it."

"What is it, Mother?" and "What is it, Louise?" Neila and Paul asked in unison. The Professor took hold of his wife's arm and tried to calm her down. "Let's go into the office and talk there," Dr. Green said, and Ofara added, "I'll get your son, Louise."

The office was large enough, but six adults and a girl filled it up to capacity. Neila and Ofara brought more chairs from another office, and Louise started talking excitedly to her son, having taken her granddaughter in her arms and put her on her knees as she sat down. Dr. Green looked on while Prof. Rodin, standing behind his wife, patted her on the shoulder in an attempt to calm her down. The younger man was looking on with a growing sense of impotence.

At last, Ofara said in a calm but decisive voice, "Please, Louise, try to tell it in a clear order, so that we understand better what we can do."

Cornell then sat on a chair beside his mother, and she held the child back to him and arranged her ruffled hair. She started talking in a low but still agitated voice.

"Clare and I decided to go to the shop and join you here later, because she wanted to ask me about getting a few things for the house." She stopped and swallowed, then added, "As we were walking around, looking at the various items to find what was suitable for the house, I noticed a few things were not in their usual place. At first I thought there were one or two that had been misplaced by careless customers, and I started putting them back; then I looked again, and thought there might be some idea behind that disorder, so I stopped rearranging them and decided to leave them where they were and ask you, Ofara, about it. Perhaps there was some meaning behind all this mess that was done by someone for a purpose. And then, it happened!"

She paused, and her husband asked sharply, "What happened?" and Cornell looked around and said with some agitation, "But where is Clare? Hasn't she come here with you?"

Louise gave her son a painful look, saying in a weak voice, "I don't know where Clare is. She vanished."

"Vanished? How? What does it mean?" But his mother just shook her head, silently, as the tears welled up in her eyes.

In the silence that ensued, Ofara asked in a calm though penetrating voice, "And you think that the items, which had been moved from their usual places, had anything to do with Clare's disappearance?"

Louis nodded and said, "That's why I'd rather you came back with me to take a look, Ofara. Maybe you can make some sense out of it. Paul," she turned to her husband, her voice controlled better now, having some plan to follow, "you take Cornell and Charm to the flat and don't leave them alone; but we don't need to go all of us to the store."

• • •

"I have returned the first two things I noticed back to where I had found them, so that if there is a system, it will look clearer to you," Louise said as her daughter and the Witch accompanied her into the curio shop. "See if you can find them out by yourselves what has been misplaced, and then you may be able to get something out of it."

"The Voodoo doll!" Neila cried out immediately. "I remember it clearly sitting on that shelf, grinning at me, and now it's gone. I don't suppose you've sold it, have you, Mother?"

"No, you're right. I've found it here, on the central table."

"Let's make a list, then," said the Witch, "and see if it makes any sense."

"But we don't know in what order to put them," Neila protested.

"First we see what they are, and the list will form itself. I'm sure of it," Ofara replied, starting to look around. "It's all right if you point them out, Louise," she told her friend, while the woman was putting the doll back on the shelf, and the girl took a piece of paper and started writing.

"The other thing I found out of place was the Amerindian feather head-dress, which used to stand at the table's center, where I saw the doll; it had been put on a chair in the corner where I could barely see it. Here." She took the object and put it back on the table, and her daughter wrote it down in the list.

"The claw necklace!" Neila said, "It's hanging on the wall! What was hanging here usually, Mother?"

"That should have been the Japanese drawing of a clown's face," said her mother. "Now, where is that?"

"Here," said Ofara as she spotted the paper scroll lying on the desk at the side of the shop.

"That's two more," said Neila, writing them down in her list, as Louise put them both back.

"How many have you got?" asked Ofara.

"Four."

"There should be at least one more," remarked the Witch.

"Why?" asked Louise.

"There should be five, or seven, or nine," Ofara said. "I can sense magic working here, and magic does not like even numbers."

Mother and daughter searched the shop until Neila said, "I have an idea that scarf was not usually here, among those clothes items, am I right, Mother?"

"The Mongolian silk scarf?" the woman came up to her, looking around. "No, you're right, it's usually shown apart, being so special."

"What's so special about it?" asked Ofara, "though I can see it's different from the other dress items."

"It's made of pure, natural Chinese silk; the other things are much more common."

"But you said it's Mongolian?"

"The story is that Mongolian highwaymen used it to strangle passing merchants in order to steal their precious possessions and merchandise."

"Wow!" said Neila, obviously impressed.

"This gives us the last clue to the meaning of the list," said the Witch, as Neila wrote that item down.

"Really?" the girl asked. "And in what order should I put them?"

"Let me see," said Ofara. "First, it must be the Voodoo doll, symbolizing a woman and a general warning, as if intending to do some Voodoo curse. Clare may have been taken not as an act against herself particularly, but as a threat against the family as a whole. Here, look at that. Those Indian feathers, as far as I can tell, belong to the golden eagle, and they have been cut. It can point out to Clare's golden hair that is going to be cut off."

"But why?" asked Louise fiercely.

"I have a feeling, as Neila has been sensing it for a while, that there is a threat against your family, and these are the initial steps to accomplish it. It starts with some mild operation, like kidnapping and hair cutting, but I suspect those threats will become more and more severe. Let's see what else we have here." The Witch looked down the list and at the items appearing there, and her face darkened by the minute.

"I don't like that at all," she said, "but I'm afraid we must know all the facts if we want to act against them. Here, for instance, is the Japanese clown with the distorted face. I'm afraid Clare's face may be cut to look like a clown's; then, as the claw necklace points out, her fingers may be pulled out, and at last she's going to be choked to death by the silk scarf."

The others looked at her with astonishment and horror. "But why should anyone do a terrible think like that? What do they want of us?" Mother and daughter asked together in a terrified voice.

"This I don't know, as I don't know who is doing that," Ofara replied in a quiet voice, not showing her own deep concern. "But I suppose we'll know soon enough. I expect we'll probably get a message telling us what would happen if that person's demands are not answered."

"What kind of demands can they be?" asked Neila.

Ofara thought for a moment, looking from her to her mother and back, thinking about the rest of the family. "What I see in you," she said slowly, "is a family who has strong inclinations toward magic, though not all of you are witches. This, together with your overall kind and helpful nature, may be an anathema to some powerful and evil character, perhaps. I can't say exactly what it is, yet, but I don't think I, or any one witch, can act alone here. You need help, that much is clear to me."

"What kind of help?" asked Louise in a weak voice.

"I need to consult other witches, some of whom have greater powers than I do," Ofara answered.

• • •

They left, finally. Louise closed the shop and the three women accompanied her to the Rodin apartment, where they found the men trying to keep calm but hardly succeeding in hiding their agitation. Paul was preparing hot drinks while Cornell was walking up and down the living room, with Charm trying in vain to attract his attention to her antics. She was on the verge of crying when the women came in, so Louise took her out of her father's arms, while Neila went to help her father serving the food.

"Please, sit down, Cornell," his mother said quietly but authoritatively. "You're not doing any good like that."

He sat down beside Ofara on the couch, and Prof. Rodin said, "What's the verdict, then?"

His wife told the men of their findings and the Witch's observations, and he said, "What kind of help do you think you'll need, Ofara. And first of all, shouldn't we call the police?"

"What could the police do?" asked Louise. "Take fingerprints? There wouldn't be any, it was all done with magic. The man was not even there!"

"Do you mean to say he got Clare by charm? Like a stage magician?" Cornell exclaimed. "Now, I can't believe that!"

"It looks like a stage magician's act," Ofara tried to explain, "but it's nothing of the sort. The man seems to be very powerful, and he didn't need to be there to affect Clare's disappearance."

The Professor looked at her with interest. "You seem to have an idea who he is," he said, calmly.

"An idea, yes," she answered, "but I need corroboration, and for that purpose I have to get in touch with a certain person."

"What kind of person, and how are you going to get in touch with them," Louise asked.

"Here, the telephone is all yours, if you need it."

"The telephone won't be much help to reach this person. He is not alive today."

"Are you going to act as a medium, then, and call up his ghost?" Neila looked at Ofara with a crooked smile playing on her face. In spite of her worry about her sister-in-law, whom she liked, she seemed to enjoy this unusual situation.

"Not at all," Ofara replied, preparing herself to concentrate her thoughts. "I intend to call him where he is still alive, some time about the Middle Ages."

"The Middle Ages!" Paul and Louise cried out, while Cornell looked at her as if she had gone out of her mind.

"I've done this sort of thing before," the Witch said, calmly. "Now, it would be better if you don't interrupt while I concentrate to get in touch with him." At that, silence fell, and Ofara, relaxing in her seat, closed her eyes and detached herself from the world around her.

In a few moments they all could see the apparition, as if in a transparent mist. He was a man in his middle age, tall and thin and a little stooped, walking along in a rather desolated place, wearing a kind of old-fashioned – not to say old looking – coat and hat, with a bag thrown on his back. He seemed absorbed in his thoughts, though once in a while waking up from them to look around him.

The man seemed to exist in a world of his own and did not pay any attention to those in the room, but Neila cried out suddenly, "Doesn't he remind you of the figurine?"

"Shshsh," her mother shushed her, and silence fell again over the apparition.

Suddenly, the man stopped and sent his gaze directly at Ofara. "You're one of them, then?" he said in a strange accent, which none except Paul and Ofara could understand.

"Hallo, Finbar. We need your help."

"That's a change!" he said. "Only once was I of real help to anyone; usually I'm the one who needs it."

"That's exactly the kind of help I need from you, against that same man you stood up to that time," the Witch said.

"You mean that evil wizard?"

"You used your music to fight against him, and now he is attacking us and we need you and your music again."

"Ha!" the Minstrel said in a self-derogating tone. "I only won because he gave up! I don't expect him to do it again."

"Still, you can give us a hint. What was it particularly that defeated that wizard? Was it only your music?"

"My music would never have done it alone, without that love between the two young people. If love is strong enough, nothing much can stand against it. Is there such love in your present case?"

"I don't know these people well enough, and I don't know anyone who can produce your kind of music."

"Well, that's what you must find to help you, there's nothing else I can do but give you that advice." The transparent figure and its surrounding began to fade out, and soon the room reverted to what it was. Ofara shook herself and opened her eyes.

"What was all this about?" asked Prof. Rodin.

She looked around her as if slowly returning to the present state of affairs, then said to Neila, "I think you're right. Even though it came from China, that flute player looks definitely like Finbar the Minstrel."

"But who is that Finbar the Minstrel and what had he done?" asked Cornell fiercely. Even after seeing the apparition, he still was not ready to believe his own eyes.

"It must have been that same wizard, who had captured the spirits of a whole family in a certain castle, and Finbar released them with the help of his music."

"But didn't he say that music was not enough?" said Prof. Rodin.

"Music and love," asserted Ofara.

"I think nothing much can contest Clare's love for her child," said Louise. "We must hope that will be our aid in getting her back from the wizard's clutches."

"But, do you mean to tell us that the same wizard that lived in the middle ages is still alive today?" asked Cornell with disbelief.

"I have an idea he has found a source of eternal life and is getting bored with himself, so he's coming up with a kind of amusement for himself."

"Well," said Louise fiercely, "we are not going to provide that evil man the source of amusement he's looking for!"

"But why us?" asked Cornell.

"I think he has a beef against witches."

"But we are not witches!" the young man protested.

"Some of you are," she pointed out, "like your sister, for instance, and perhaps others, not aware of it yet."

"Others?" he looked around him with a questioning glare. At that moment, little Charm, who had been playing with some artifacts from the shop, pulled at his sleeve and said in a complaining voice, "Daddy, I want Mummy. Where is she?"

"We are trying to find her, darling," he said, lifting her on to his knees.

"She gone?" the child asked, then added, "I help find Mummy, Daddy."

"Yes, honey," he said, caressing her face lightly with his finger, not paying attention to what she was saying. Then, noticing Ofara and Neila staring at him and Charm, he asked, belligerently, "What!"

They said nothing, continuing to stare, and he called out, "No! You don't think so! That's impossible!"

"What is it all about?" asked Paul, and Louise said, "Charm? Well, I never!"

"Well," said Neila, "she's my niece, after all, and it is in the family."

"But she's too young to be of any real help!" the grandmother exclaimed, and the father added, "Not on your life! She's far too young. "

"We'll have to find out, if it's the only thing we can do," Ofara said, calmly.


## III

Clare woke up from her blackout, stunned and confused. She looked around her with blurred eyes, trying to figure out what had happened and where she was. A large figure loomed over her, but it did not stay still, its lines continually moving and changing. Finding herself sitting on an unfamiliar chair, she tried to get up but was unable to, as if tied and bound hand and foot.

"You'd better sit still, or you may hurt yourself," a gruff voice said, but she could not tell where it came from, as it rolled round the place like thunder.

"Why?" she said, defiantly, "what do you want of me, and who are you, anyway? I can't even see you clearly!"

Coarse laughter burst out of the changing figure opposite her, and she automatically tried in vain to move away. "You don't know me?" a voice said inside the laughter; "I am the great Kindrik the Wizard!" and another peel of thunder accompanied that announcement.

"Kindrik the Wizard, what a funny appellation!" said Clare, forgetting her trouble for a moment. "Like a stage magician. Is that what you are?"

"Do you think I brought you here by stage magic!" the voice roared around her, and in spite of herself Clare cringed. "I am the greatest wizard ever lived! I have lived for hundred of years and now, at the peak of my power, I prepare for my greatest deed ever!" he bellowed.

Clare was silent. What could she say to such declaration? All she wanted was to get out of that horrible place, back home to the comfort of her husband's love and her daughter's cheerfulness.

"Well, what do you say to that?" the unclear figure of the wizard demanded, as if in need of her acquiescence.

"I suppose that you are, but what has it got to do with me? I am of no importance to you in any way."

"You may not know it but, you see, I must go after all the witches in the world. They have had their fun long enough, with their silly charms and their false magic. Now, I am going to destroy them! Destroy them all, you hear!"

"All right, all right," Clare tried to pacify the agitated wizard, "but what has that to do with me? I am not a witch!"

"Much you know about it," he replied, his vague figure moving swiftly around the place.

Her sight clarified somewhat, and now she could see better what was in the room. It looked like a large vault, with such a high, dark ceiling she could barely see it, only had an idea that it was in the shape of a dome. The whole place looked like an enormous cavern, though she could trace the shape of the stones the walls had been built of. But it was dark like a cave, lit only by some kind of magic lanterns. 'Louise could use them in her shop,' Clare reflected, absentmindedly. There were many objects there that she thought Louise would be happy to have in her store, but many of them were too strange for Clare to know there names or purpose. 'Are they all used for magic making?' she asked herself.

"No," she said, "I am not a witch, though I am interested in magic. It is my sister-in-law who has some powers, I don't know of what kind, though; and that woman, Ofara..."

"Ah!" he interrupted her, "That creature! I know about her and she is in for a sad end for all her mischief! But it is in your family as well, for what about your own mother? I remember her – "

"But my mother has been dead some years now," Clare said, sadly, "so – "

"And if you think you haven't inherited some of her power, you're really a sad creature indeed!" the Wizard said with such contempt that made her cringe again. "I can see it in your mind, but you're afraid of it, clinging to your husband and daughter." For a moment, he sunk in deep reflection, as if the mention of Clare's daughter had awakened some idea in him.

Still, he dismissed it, as Clare said, "I'm not afraid, but my husband –"

"I know, he does not believe in magic! He is really in for a great game, for which he is not really prepared!" and he burst out in his horrible laughter again. "But that's enough idle talk. I'm not going to give you a chance to fight me at all, you hear!"

At that, he made a sweeping movement with his arms, and a large globe appeared, made of some kind of a milky glass; it floated above Clare's head, and she looked at it with glaring eyes, a real fear growing in her heart. The Wizard began an incantation, and Clare felt something tearing inside her; she felt herself going, breaking away, her main essence detaching itself from her body... There was an unspeakable darkness which wrapped her vision, everything was vanishing from around her, nothing was left but a blank void. She lost her consciousness again. Her limbs relaxed and her whole body slumped in the chair, while inside the milky glass of the globe a shape appeared. Clare's soul, deprived of its body, unable to function away from it, looked down at the paralyzed figure with a sense of utter impotence and despair.

• • •

As darkness fell, the Rodin family together with Ofara the Witch bundled into Louise's car and went to the young people's house in the suburb, where Cornell put the sleeping child to bed; Neila and Ofara were invited to stay the night. The elder Rodins planned to return later to their flat in town, but for the time being the whole family stayed together. They assembled in the dining corner of the living room and had some kind of a snack meal, then moved to a more comfortable sitting on couches and armchairs, having coffee and trying to initiate a council of war.

Nothing much came of it as they had very little idea of either what they were actually against, or how to fight it; they only agreed that Ofara should get in touch with any of the witches she thought could help. After a while, the older couple left to go back home, and Cornell showed Ofara and Neila to their rooms. For a long time Ofara lay awake, vaguely watching lights from outside peering through her window, playing among the swaying tree branches to create blurred shapes on the walls of her room; later, a sickle moon rose in the east and defused its wan glow, before she fell at last into a fitful sleep.

It did not last long. Whether it was the strange bed or the uncomfortable feeling that had been plaguing her throughout the day, the Witch woke suddenly in the middle of the night, not sure at first what was wrong.

In a moment, she knew what had wakened her up. A deep darkness had fallen over the house, and she could no longer see the street lights, or the moon that should have climbed over the tree tops. Lying in bed and reflecting what she should do, Ofara heard Neila's voice whispering at her door. The Witch rose and opened it, feeling the heavy darkness weighing on her chest like a load of lead.

"Go and get dressed and I'll do the same," she whispered to the young woman; "I'll meet you in the living room."

"What should we do?" the young witch asked the older woman, as they met again.

"I think we should let him make the first move," Ofara said. She then produced her bag, which seemed to contain some things not usually carried by women. She pulled out a large candle, made it stand on the coffee table by itself and lit it, not with a match but with a few words of incantation and a movement of the hand. The light made the surroundings soft gray, not so oppressive; the two women were able now to make some hot drinks, with which they sat down to talk and think together.

Not for long, though, because very soon the silence was broken by sharp noises, the banging of things that began flying around the room.

"Ouch!" the novice witch cried out in pain and alarm, as some heavy object hit her on the side of the head.

"Come quickly," Ofara pulled her by the arm, and they dove together out of the way behind a couch. "Let me see," she whispered, turning Neila's head toward her.

"It's nothing, I have a strong head," the younger woman whispered back. "But, can't you stop it, Ofara?"

"Only make that object tantrum milder. My powers are more with people than artifacts."

"Then shouldn't you contact the brain behind it and try to influence it?"

"I don't know enough about that wizard, only that he's extremely strong," Ofara replied with a twist of her mouth. "But I'll try, see what I can do." She closed her eyes in concentration, and after a while she said, "I can't find him anywhere; he seems to be hiding behind a kind of barrier that feels as strong as a wall of stones."

Then she added, "But let's join our powers together this time, and try harder. I know you're just an apprentice, but you do have powers, if not yet fully developed and perhaps not well directed. Still, if you concentrate on what you have learned, and follow my thoughts as you can feel them, together we may be able to have a better effect on this magic."

"I'm not quite as sure of myself as you are but I'll try." The two witches then concentrated together. From Ofara's mind Neila picked up an incantation, in which she joined; as they pronounced it together, their combined voice became stronger and stronger, until at last it overcame the strange noises in the house. In a short while things calmed down and objects stopped flying about; they finally fell down to the floor and on furniture, creating a mess in the nicely ordered room. Only once in a while some objects or other would jump up in a fit or a jerk, demonstrating the existence of the wizard's power but to much less effect than before.

At last, Neila breathed a deep sigh. "Well, that was something! I've never done anything like that before."

They came out from behind the sofa, cleared it from some kitchen utensils and a few broken ornaments then sat on it. "I'd like to go and see about Charm and Cornell now, shouldn't I?" Neila said. "Why d'you think they haven't stirred with all that commotion?"

"I'm not sure," Ofara replied. "I wonder if the Wizard was concentrating on the two of us, the acknowledged witches, in particular."

"The darkness is still there, you know. I can feel it, even if it's more gray than black. What should we do about that?"

"Nothing. I have an idea it will lift by itself at day break," Ofara said, decisively.

They did not go back to bed but stayed up in the living room. Neila had left the couch for Ofara to stretch on and she did the same in a comfortable double chair, and they managed to catch some sleep before the gray dawn peeped from the window. In their sleep, as if part of a dream, they both could feel the heavy, unnatural darkness lifting away from the house, leaving behind the fading street lights to awaken the day.

• • •

Ofara woke up properly as the first rays of the sun peeped through a window. She rose and stretched, went to wash, then came into the kitchen. Having made coffee, she woke up Neila, and they had a hot drink before setting out to clear the living room of the mess. They had put back a great number of objects in their places and got rid of some broken ones when Cornell appeared in the room with Charm on his arms.

"What is it? What's been happening here?" He asked, looking around at the half-disordered room. "Did you have a party last night? You're wounded, Neila!"

"Didn't you hear the commotion?" asked Ofara, and Neila said, "You're lucky, you and Charm. We had a hell of a night!"

The child said then, "Where's Mummy?" and Neila took her in her arms, kissed and hugged her.

"Let's have breakfast and we'll tell you all about it," the Witch suggested.

Before finishing the story the phone rang, and Neila took it. "Yes, Mother – No, Mother – You did? – I think Ofara'd better tell you about it –" and she handed the instrument over. Ofara listened, interjected a few words and put it down.

"Louise says we are all to meet at the Hecate's Place. You're not going to work today, are you, Cornell?"

"Not in this situation, no. I must look after the child, there is no time to get a sitter at this hour of the morning."

"And it would be wrong to involve an innocent by-stander," added his sister.

"Aren't we innocent by-standers?" he asked, more harshly perhaps than he meant.

"Not at all. We are a family of witches, want it or not, brother, and the fight is directly against us and no one else!"

'The girl has guts,' Ofara thought. 'I hope it won't go wrong for her in this fight.'

They cleared breakfast, and when father and daughter went to get dressed, Ofara said to Neila, "I would like you to get me an intimate article of your sister-in-law, to help get in touch with her."

The girl went and came back, showing the Witch a pair of golden earrings set with clear, light blue, aquamarine stones. "Are these any good?"

"Perfect, if she wears them habitually."

"Almost all the time, and I'm quite surprised she didn't have them on when she was kidnapped," was the reply.

Cornell appeared again with a spare key for the shop, just in case they were getting there first. But there was no chance of that, as Louise and Paul had acted in a hurry and were in the store when the others arrived in Cornell's car.

Louise took them to the back room and they all sat down, preparing for some serious talk.

"How's the shop doing?" Ofara asked, as if in a preliminary. She had not much use for such knick-knacks as filled the place, depending more on Elinor's specialized supply for the necessary magical objects.

"Some of my acquaintances are not too particular whether what they buy here is the genuine article or a pretty imitation, as long as it looks right," Louise replied with a wry smile, as if jeering at herself for some shoddy dealings.

"Dr. Green would know, though, wouldn't he?" commented her husband, dryly. He knew that the Museum could not afford half the stuff in it, but needed some rich and powerful patrons, who acted in anonymity to supply it with its treasures.

"Forget it," Louis said in a commanding voice. "We have more important business right now, and first of all getting Clare back. Now, Ofara, tell us what we can do about it?"

"First, I'll try again to find her, both physically and mentally." She extended her hand to Neila, who put the earrings in it; Ofara closed her fist over them, then closed her eyes in concentration. The others sat around the room, silently watching the Witch in her action.

The trace of the young woman's spirit in her ornaments was very strong, as well as its connection with the people in the room; in particular, the Witch felt it with the child, hearing her silent voice calling "Mummy, Mummy!" as if she knew what Ofara was trying to do.

The Witch thought the conditions for finding Clare should be favorable enough, but as much effort as she put into the search, as much as she stretched her powers of human touch, she was unable to sense any trace of Clare's actual existence. It was not as if the young woman was not there, but the feeling of a very strong wall blocking her mental view told Ofara she would need more powers, different from her own, to help her reach Clare.

As her mind was returning back from the search, Ofara heard Neila cry out; she opened her eyes and saw Cornell taking hold of his daughter; hugging her tight, he was saying, "What's happened? What's wrong with Charm? She seemed to have fainted!" He did not seem to notice that in his fright, he was using her proper, magical name for the very first time.

"I don't think anything's wrong with her," Ofara said. Turning to Louise, she added, "You can check up on her but I think she's all right. She simply has enormous powers, which are very rare at her age, and she's not exactly aware of what she's doing."

"What d'you mean?" asked the grandmother, "what's happened?" She looked from father to daughter with consternation.

"She was there, with me, feeling that strong wall that separated us from her mother," Ofara answered.

"What is that wall?" asked the Professor. "Do you know where she is, then?"

"The locality is not as important as the conditions she's in," the Witch said quietly. "I don't have the power to break through such mental wall, I'm afraid that wizard is stronger than me." She pondered for a moment then said, "It's time for me to call for help, because it is very clear I cannot do this alone."

"Do you know who to call, then?" asked Cornell, still holding Charm as if he would not let her go anywhere.

"I think we should divide our strength in two directions. One should be Professor Rodin."

"What can I do?" asked Paul, quietly.

"You should access your computer at the University and extract as much information about that wizard as you can; he calls himself Kindrik, and you should find him in Medieval Europe. Also try his connection with Finbar the Minstrel; that should take you in the right direction."

"Were you able at all to have a look at the Wizard?" asked Louise, as Paul got up to go to the College.

"He is unapproachable, I'm afraid, and I'm not sure he's quite human," Ofara said; "Hundreds of years ago he was still a real person; but having lived for so long, having absorbed so much power and knowledge from all kinds of sources – some of them definitely inhuman – I think it must have affected his whole being and now there is very little of humanity left in him. I don't think we can ever overcome him with simple means, magical or otherwise."

"What, then?"

"We'll have to combine all our powers to work together on different levels. That's my idea, and for that purpose I'm going to get in touch now with a head of a coven I know, so she can bring some of her people to do the work."

"All right," said Louise, as Paul was closing the store's door behind him, "Do it, then."

"Here goes!" said Ofara; and, as the door closed behind the Professor, she closed her eyes.

## IV

The witches came shortly after noon. The Rodin family, older and younger, together with Ofara, was still sitting in the back room of the Hecate's Place. When Paul had come back from the University they had a light lunch there, almost exhausting the supply in the small fridge.

"Well, Ofara, you wanted us and here we are," said a woman older than Ofara; she was tall and gray looking, and her eyes shone like lightning. She was accompanied by two other witches, who looked with interest at the family members congregated in the small room, one of them acknowledging Neila.

"Karlina!" said the Ofara, "so good of you to come!" She presented the newcomers and the family members to each other, including the child who immediately attracted their attention.

Karlina, the coven's leader, explained that she and each of her companions had their own special powers, as they thought might be important in this particular case. She herself had specialized as a Weather witch, which demanded the greatest powers a witch could have.

Vanger, the only man among them, was fair-haired and solid looking; his powers were only second to those of the Weather witch, connected as they were with the Earth and earthly materials, buildings, and other inanimate objects. The third witch, Sarit – a slight, youngish woman of medium height with soft, light brown hair and hazel green eyes – specialized in magical artifacts, the sort of powers most witches aspired to have at the beginning of their training.

With all these people crowding in it now, the small backroom behind the store looked even smaller, and Karlina turned to Vanger with a knowing look. The man made a movement with his arm and murmured a few words, and suddenly there was room enough, with enough furniture for everyone to sit in comfort. Using merely her gaze to silence the astonished cries of the family members, Karlina turned to the Professor.

"Well, Paul, we've known each other time enough to realize what is necessary. I'm sure you've looked up this business and can tell us something about it."

"Have you heard about that wizard, Kindrik?" he asked.

"Not too much, and I don't mind hearing more from you, so that all of us can learn what we are up against."

"Well, he appears in writings from different sources of different periods, enough to think there may have been various people of the same name; on the other hand, there are some indications that it is all about one and the same person, as unlikely as it sounds. He has not always been vicious, but always wanted more power than he should have had legitimately. More than anything else, he aspired to rule over everything: people, land, events, or anything else you may think of. This desire had caused him to become more and more brutal in his dealings, and less and less caring for human life, as he had advanced in years and gathered more and more power."

"What is he after now, then?" asked Vanger.

"Witches. He has developed a thing against witches and that's why he is after our family; it seems that we consist of more than the average number of people with one kind of powers or another."

"Oh?" the sorcerer wondered, looking them all over. Sarit opened her eyes wide, absorbing the sight around her and said, "How is it, then, that besides Neila, none of you is known to us as an active witch?"

"I don't even believe in magic!" Cornell grumbled for the umpteenth time, looking with some resentment at his twin sister.

"There's a person missing from this meeting, isn't it so, Ofara? Your wife, Mr. Rodin?" Karlina addressed the young man. "I don't know if you ever knew her mother, because she died when Clare was still too young to remember; but she was a dear friend of mine and a very talented witch. You must have heard of her, Sarit, Vanger – Garnet, she was called among us, though I think she had a different name among non witches. Eh, Cornell?" she said gently to him, as if parting with an unwelcome secret.

"I never heard that Clare's mother was a witch," he mumbled.

"And a very clever one," Karlina assured him. "She began to specialized in stones, precious and semiprecious ones, and it was she who had bought Clare these lovely earrings you are holding now, Ofara, knowing their affinity to her daughter's character."

"Well," said Louise, who was listening with a mixture of interest and impatience. "Saving Clare and defeating that vicious wizard is the task at hand, so let's see what can be done to accomplish all that as soon as possible. Eh, Karlina?"

"You're absolutely right, Louise," the Witch turned to her in a familiar way that seemed rather unusual, but perhaps fit the circumstances. "The three of us must find out the physical situation of the kidnapping, only then we can decide what to do. Ofara, can you lead us to the Wizard's place of action, as you've been there before?"

Some changes in the sitting arrangement were then performed, as the four experienced witches got together in one corner of the room. They sat down on the floor in a circle, and having practiced eye contact that expressed their mental approach to each other, they closed their eyes and concentrated. After a short while they came back to the present, and Karlina said, "Vanger, what did you see?"

"I saw a high, rugged mountain, and a sort of castle built close to its top with some of the local stones and boulders. It looks like an integral part of the rocky ground around it, well embedded in the earth, affecting it with its magical properties. It seems very hard to penetrate, and I'll need all my powers to work against it."

"Are you up to it, though?" asked his Chief.

"I should hope so," the man answered with a quiet confidence.

"All right. Now Sarit, what did you see?"

"I looked inside that habitation that Vanger described, and my mental vision was attracted to the many magical artifacts inside. They are interesting and powerful, but the most important is a globe of milky glass that seems to contain a woman's soul; it is floating in the air over her lifeless body, presenting such a pathetic sight …"

"That's Clare's," said Ofara. "I sensed her essence last night, but was unable to penetrate the castle and see her. Nevertheless, I do hope to be able to reach her, because though trapped and dormant, she still emits the strong sense of love and yearning that connects her to her family."

"Good," said Karlina, and fell into a momentary meditation. "Now," she said as she stirred again, "while this Kindrik has accumulated an overwhelming power of magic during the centuries, it seems that at the same time his power of thinking and reasoning has diminished."

"How do you figure?" asked Prof. Rodin.

"Well, look at what he has been doing with that power, and what his ambition is! On the one hand, he's kidnapped Clare and made a coherent plan to assault her; but on the other, he's also planning to attack us here. How is he going to do both tasks together, while also guarding Clare from being discovered and released? I think, without realizing it, he's given us a great advantage."

"Have you, then, thought up how we are going to go about it?" asked Sarit.

"It's going to be like that," answered the Coven Leader. "Sarit, you take charge of the magical artifacts in the store here. I'm sure Kindrik is going to make use of them in one way or another. Ofara, you will guard the minds of the family members against any influence the Wizard may try to exert on them. Sometimes, mental attack may be enough to defeat an enemy right away. I shall keep watch on any outside effect the wizard may use – the atmosphere forms a great possibility as a battle ground. Vanger, you will get over to the castle and start working on destroying it. When Kindrik fights us here, he won't be able to guard his castle, and I don't think any magical power he had imbued it with can stand on its own against your own very extensive one."

"But what shall I do when I get into the castle? My power over people and their minds is rather limited."

"You'll take with you Clare's husband, Cornell, who would act with his love for his wife to free her."

"Me! How? I told you I don't even believe in magic!" The man cried out with agitation.

"But you do believe in love, don't you? Clare needs you, and you would rescue her with the power of your love for her."

"I wouldn't know how." he said in anguish.

"Neila will come with you, and you'll work together. She's had some basic, general training in magic that should help with whatever kind of power necessary at the moment; all you have to do is concentrate on reaching Clare's soul that is trapped inside the globe. Both of you together must be able to free and return it to Clare's inanimate body, then carry her back to us here."

• • •

The plan was set and, as Karlina said they should not separate again until it was all over, they all spent the night together in Hecate's Place; Vanger conjured a couple of mattresses that were put on the floor for those who had no room left on couches and chairs. The Leader Witch stipulated that the best time for Vanger, Cornell and Neila to move their spirits toward the castle would be if and when they felt the Wizard's presence in their vicinity, so that they could perform their action without his notice. The child was to be left in the care of her grandparents, Louise and Paul Rodin. They were all to be sleeping in their clothes, ready for action in a few minutes.

The trouble started in the early hours of the morning. Ofara, sleeping light, heard a stir among the magical artifacts in the store and woke the other witches and Cornell. Vanger, Neila and Cornell sat together in a corner of the backroom, concentrating on leaving their bodies and going in the direction of the castle. The child and her grandparents were left asleep in another corner; there was no point in waking them before they were needed. Ofara and Karlina sat at the center of the room, waiting for the Wizard's performance.

Sarit, who had slept inside the store, also heard the movement among the artifacts, put the light on and looked around. At first, she was rather amused at the antics of these objects, which started moving in a strange, dance-like performance, not looking dangerous at all. Some of them were life-like figurines, human and animal shapes; others were just artifacts and ornaments, like necklaces and rings, brooches in various shapes, or magic tools like candles. They seemed to come alive as if waking from sleep, stretching their limbs or bodies; they walked about the shop and looked around them, while interacting among themselves. Sarit was watching them at first in some amusement, not sensing danger.

The situation looked more troublesome when these animals started growing larger and larger. First they were the size of small pets that were getting out of hand, needing only better discipline; that in itself was becoming out of Sarit's range of powers, and for a moment she felt at a loss. From the start the creatures were also emitting noises, which did not sound very loud when they were small. Now that they were growing, these sounds also became more and more alarming; she knew they must be awakening the people at the back room, and half hoped these could come to her help in controlling all those beasts, humans, and the inanimate object which were moving by themselves.

Overwhelmed, Sarit was now rooted in her place while the enlarged, enlivened artifacts were in uproar. At the backroom, Ofara was trying to control the minds of the people, whose minds were filled with dread and panic. Suddenly, in the midst of all that commotion, Sarit heard Ofara's voice, "Don't be alarmed, they are all an illusion; the Wizard is working on your minds, not on the artifacts. Try to think them back to their natural size."

Illusion? Her fear was very real but she made an enormous effort to subdue it, visualizing the creatures back to their small size. It worked, after a while, though they were still moving about; but that part was within range of her power and she started by sending them back to their places. It was not a simple task, because there were so many of them, and some seemed to be not only independent but also intent on doing mischief.

One stone necklace flew about the shop and landed on Louise's neck, choking her out of breath, and Sarit had to exert a great force to release it. It fell to the floor and continued to twist like a snake that has been hurt, hitting and emitting drops of poison. Then a tiny human hunter sent his spear flying and it hit Paul in the arm that was holding Charm, until he almost dropped the child for the pain. There was no doubt the Wizard was working not only on their minds to create illusions, but also on the artifacts themselves.

One of the illusions, though, seemed to refuse to grow small again. In her concentration to help Sarit and the others fight against their faulty thoughts, Ofara heard a cry of fear. As she opened her eyes, she realized that in front of her was standing not a miniature animal but a full scale lion, crouching in his intention to jump at them.

"Stop!" she cried out at him. He froze in place, and she had a chance to examine his mind. He was indeed a real lion and not of the artifacts. "What are you and where do you come from?" she asked without words, addressing his very mind.

"That bloody wizard turned me into a toy!" he growled; "and now I'm going to have my revenge."

"If you have your revenge and devour us," the Witch said reasonably, "then you'll be killed and no one will help you going back home."

"Help? You can help me?"

"Show me the place you've come from, what you remember of it," she commanded. The next moment she saw a great savannah with high grass, a few trees and a reflection of water. She closed her eyes and murmured and incantation. "There!"

The lion was gone! Charm clapped her hands and Louise cried out, "Ofara! Did you just send that lion back to Africa?"

"Come," she said instead of an answer, "let's help Sarit control those artifacts in the shop."

• • •

On the mountain side, close to its top, Vanger's spirit was checking around the impregnable looking castle. Neila's and Cornell's spirits were hovering about, not sure what they should do. Neila was holding Cornell, whose disbelief in magic hampered him in his effort. The communication between the three could only be mental, and Cornell had no experience in that at all.

"What'd you think?" Neila asked Vanger after a little while.

"The ground of both the castle and the slope is saturated with centuries' use of magic," he answered.

"Can you overcome it?"

He nodded, having no doubt of the fact, only measuring the amount of effort he would have to put into it. It was lucky the Wizard was foolish enough to leave the castle on its own while attacking the witches in town, relying on that old magic alone. As powerful as it was, Vanger's own power was drawn directly from the earth, and he had years of experience using it.

He started his incantations. Having signed to the others to stay at some distance from him, he let his spirit fly beyond the boundaries of the influence of magic. He then gathered his strength from the pure soil, and from the rock underneath, turned toward the castle and swooped at its invisible magical walls. These were heavy and looked tightly bound, no signs of cracks in them. Lines of energy in the form of lightning started shooting from Vanger's spirit at the stones in the walls, hitting at single spots. Some time passed, and much energy was spent, until the first single thread of split showed. Neila pointed it out to Cornell, and both felt as if they were holding their breath.

More cracks appeared, revealing the original blue lines of the pure magic used by the Wizard. Gradually, signs of the brown and yellow hues of the earth could be spotted; they slowly grew red hot, then burned bright crimson. Vanger's red and Kindrik's blue fought against each other, then combined and intermingled. Vanger's spirit looked squashed with the effort; loud noise arose from the conflicting colors, high and piercing, until they became unbearable. The air shook around the castle, then the energy lightning softened; the mixed blue and red turned unified purple that took over the walls of magic; then it melted away, leaving the castle's physical walls standing naked.

Neila, who followed the proceedings with her mind, felt the mental act of breathing and asked, "What now?"

"Now we shall have no trouble filtering inside through the physical wall with our minds," Vanger said as he led the way.

"Through the walls?" Cornell was still clinging to his disbelief.

"We are only here in spirit, don't forget," Vanger explained patiently. "There is no need for any physical action. Let's get in and find out what condition your wife is in."

He led the way and Neila came after him, while Cornell lagged behind as if afraid of what he might find inside. "Now, you must look for Clare, Brother; try to sense her with your feelings," his sister encouraged him.

"I have no idea how to do such a thing," he answered.

"Let your love for her guide you," said Vanger. "Think about closing your mental eyes and concentrating."

Cornell tried to do that, then he felt that visualizing the figure of Clare helped him sense her location. Soon he was in the same room as her actual body, where it was sitting limp on a chair, with a large, semi- transparent sphere hovering above her head.

"What is this?" he whispered mentally, pointing toward the shaded form inside the globe.

"That's her soul," his sister answered. "That bastard separated her spirit from her body, that's why she seems paralyzed."

"What can I do, then?"

"Send her your love, in any way you know."

Cornell's spirit brought to his mind all his forms of love for Clare, using all the endearing phrases he could think and feel. "I can feel her!" he suddenly whispered, and again intensified his effort. But it was all in vain, Clare's soul could not be freed from the sphere. While the man and the two witches were beginning to feel desperate, another spiritual figure appeared suddenly, the small form of a child.

"Charm!" Neila and Cornell shouted in one voice. "What are you doing here, child?" Neila cried, and Cornell's spirit tried to scoop up his daughter's bodiless shape. "How did you get here?" he asked, frustrated by his ineffective movements and hovering in agitation around the girl's form.

Instead of answering, the little girl cried out, "Mummy!" Then they saw her stretching her arms, and in her hands they noticed the little Chinese figurine of the dancing man with the flute and the crane. Fine, sweet music started flowing, the crane flapped its wings, and the shade inside the globe gradually clarified. Clare's soul began moving to the music, swirling round and round, faster and faster, until it hit the globe, which broke and splintered; Clare's spirit then flew out and at the still body on the chair. In a moment, the woman sat up and opened her eyes, saw the spirits hovering around her and stretched her arms toward her husband and child.

"Let's go now, quickly!" Vanger's spirit called in their minds. In one swift movement they were all gone back to Hecate's Place, the spirits carrying Clare's body between them.

• • •

The curio store was in state of great chaos. Sarit and Ofara, with the help of the non-magical couple Louise and Paul Rodin, were still trying their best to control the animated artifacts, when a storm had broken over the house. It was of a kind none of them had ever seen or experienced before, as all branches of Nature seemed to have taken part in it. Heavy, dark clouds covered the sky; lightning and thunder flew among them, filling the atmosphere with burning fire, deafening noise and a charge of electricity; heavy precipitations fell, a mixture of rain, snow and hale swept by raging winds, hitting everything in their path. Bricks and blocks from buildings, stones from pavements, glass from windows and trees from everywhere were flying in all directions. The house was shaking and rocking, threatening to falter; the world seemed to be coming to its end.

Vanger took immediate charge in trying to stabilize the house, as Karlina was nowhere to be seen; her colleagues assumed she was right at the center of the storm, having turned herself into pure energy to fight her battle against the Wizard. All other witches began using their mental powers to help and support their battling mate.

"What shall we do about Clare?" Cornell asked as he sat his wife gently in a chair. The woman slumped lifeless, her limbs lax and falling to the floor; only her slow, shallow breaths showed her still alive.

In the midst of all the noise and the racket, then, a soft, sweet sound was heard; in the midst of the circle of witches, Charm was standing, holding in her hands the Chinese statuette.

"How the –" Paul cried, and Louise took hold of her granddaughter. "Do you make it play, child?" she asked, softly.

"Dance!" the girl chuckled. The tune, starting soft and almost inaudible, grew louder and louder. The man's upraised foot stamped, then his other rose, and he was dancing to the sound of the flute he was playing. The crane flapped her wings, lifted her legs, and joined in the dance.

Enchanted by the magical sight and sound, none of them noticed Clare until her husband cried out, "Look! She's back!"

As if to the sound of the music, Clare was gradually sitting up in her chair, looking around her with astonishment, as if waking from a long sleep. The child stood opposite her mother, stretching the figurine at her with the playing and dancing man and crane. As the music grew louder, its sound began rivaling that of the storm outside. Suddenly, a deafening explosion was heard, an instant flash burst inside the room, and Karlina appeared, standing in her full height and glory, cloaked in glowing light. Slowly it faded, and the Witch had assumed her normal, human form. Only her eyes still glittered under her gray brows, like blazing lightning among the gray clouds.

At last the noise ceased, and Vanger said in his quiet voice, "Well?"

"Have you seen the explosion?" she asked in return.

"Was that the Wizard?" asked Ofara.

"He will not bother us again, or anyone else for that matter."

"Did the music help you?" asked Paul as he took his quivering granddaughter in his large arms, holding her tight to his body. "I wonder if he was reminded of his early experience with Finbar the Minstrel and he couldn't take it again."

"So he exploded?" Neila asked in disbelief.

"It seems there's a limit even to what a great wizard can suffer," her mother replied with a crooked smile. "Now, what'd you think? Should we keep this lovely 'Music Man' to ourselves, or take it back to the Museum? After all, it seemed to have found its true function with us."

• • •